"十三五"国家重点出版规划项目

# 李白诗歌全集英译
A Complete Edition of Pai Li's Poems in Chinese and English
With Annotations

赵彦春 译·注
Translated and Annotated by Yanchun Chao

第五卷
Volume V

上海大学出版社
·上海·

# 卷 五

# 目 录
## Contents

1003 **古近体诗三十四首**
Old-new Rhythmic Poetry, 34 Poems

1005 秋日鲁郡尧祠亭上宴别杜补阙范侍御
A Farewell Party to Remonstrant Tu and Royal Servant Fan at Mound Shrine Kiosk in Lu on an Autumn Day

1007 别鲁颂
Goodbye to Sung Lu

1009 别中都明府兄
Farewell to Brother, Magistrate of Mid-town

1010 梦游天姥吟留别
My Dream of Mt. Sky Mum: To Go or Not to Go

1014 留别曹南群官之江南
Going South, Farewell to the Officials in Ts'aonan

1019 留别于十一兄逖裴十三游塞垣
Farewell to Brother Yü Eleven and P'ei Thirteen at the Great Wall

1022 留别王司马嵩
Farewell to Commander Sung Wang

1024 夜别张五
Farewell to Chang Five at Night

1026 魏郡别苏明府因北游
Farewell to Magistrate Su at Way's Capital to Tour North

1029 留别西河刘少府
Farewell to Sheriff Liu of Westriver

| 1032 | 颍阳别元丹丘之淮阳<br>Farewell to Redknoll Yüan, Who's Leaving for Huaishine from Yingshine |
|---|---|
| 1035 | 留别广陵诸公<br>A Poem for Friends in Broadridge |
| 1038 | 广陵赠别<br>Farewell to Broadridge |
| 1039 | 感时留别从兄徐王延年从弟延陵<br>Farewell to My Cousins, Yannien, Lord of Hsu, and Track Hills |
| 1045 | 别储邕之剡中<br>Leaving for Shan, Farewell to Yung Ch'u |
| 1047 | 留别金陵诸公<br>A Poem for My Friends in Gold Hill |
| 1049 | 口号<br>An Oral Impromptu |
| 1050 | 金陵酒肆留别<br>Farewell in a Wine Shop in Gold Hill |
| 1051 | 金陵白下亭留别<br>Farewell at White Bower in Gold Hill |
| 1052 | 别东林寺僧<br>Farewell to the Monk at East Wood Temple |
| 1053 | 窜夜郎于乌江留别宗十六璟<br>Farewell to Tsung Sixteen at the Crow River When I'm Exiled to Nightboy |
| 1056 | 留别龚处士<br>Farewell to Kung, Member of Staff |
| 1058 | 赠别郑判官<br>Farewell, a Verse to Judge Cheng |
| 1059 | 黄鹤楼送孟浩然之广陵<br>Seeing Off Haojan Meng to Broadridge at Yellow Crane Tower |
| 1060 | 将游衡岳过汉阳双松亭留别族弟浮屠谈皓<br>Farewell to My Cousins Buddha and T'anhao, Passing Two-Pine Pavilion in Hanshine on the Way to Mt. Scale |

| | | |
|---|---|---|
| 1063 | 留别贾舍人至二首 | |

1063 留别贾舍人至二首
Farewell to Secretary Chia, Two Poems

1068 渡荆门送别
Farewell at Mt. Chastegate

1069 闻李太尉大举秦兵百万出征东南懦夫请缨冀申一割之用半道病还留别金陵崔侍御十九韵
Marshal Li Commands a Million Royal Troops to March Southeast and I Request for an Assignment to Do My Bit. Ill, I Write This Farewell Verse to Royal Servant Ts'ui, Prefect of Gold Hill

1073 别韦少府
Farewell to Sheriff Wei

1075 南陵别儿童入京
Leaving Southridge for the Capital, Goodbye to My Children

1077 别山僧
Farewell to a Hill Monk

1079 赠别王山人归布山
Farewell to Wang the Hermit When I Go Back to Mt. Cloth

1081 江夏别宋之悌
Farewell to Chiht'i Sung from Riversummer

1083 **古近体诗二十一首**
Old-new Rhythmic Poetry, 21 Poems

1085 南阳送客
Farewell to Southshine

1086 送张舍人之江东
Seeing Off Secretary Chang to the East

1087 送王屋山人魏万还王屋（并序）
Seeing Off Wan Way, Hermit of Mt. Kinghouse Back to Kinghouse (With a Foreword)

1099 送当涂赵少府赴长芦
Seeing Off Chao, Sheriff of Tangt'u, to Long Reed

1101 送友人寻越中山水
Seeing Off My Friend to Mid-Yüeh

| 1103 | 送族弟凝之滁求婚崔氏<br>Seeing Off a Cousin of Mine to Make a Proposal to Miss Ts'ui |
|---|---|
| 1104 | 送友人游梅湖<br>Seeing Off My Friend to Lake Wintersweet |
| 1105 | 送崔十二游天竺寺<br>Seeing Off Ts'ui Twelve to Visit Temple of Bamboo Divine |
| 1107 | 送杨山人归天台<br>Seeing Off Yang, a Hermit, to Mt. Heaven |
| 1109 | 送温处士归黄山白鹅峰旧居<br>Seeing Off Wen, a Hermit, to His Old Residence at White Goose Peak of Mt. Yellow |
| 1112 | 送方士赵叟之东平<br>Seeing Off Chao to East Peace |
| 1114 | 送韩准裴政孔巢父还山<br>Seeing Off Ch'un Han, Cheng P'ei, and Ch'aofu Kung Back to the Hills |
| 1117 | 送杨少府赴选<br>Seeing Off Yang, a County Sheriff, to His Appointment |
| 1120 | 对雪奉饯任城六父秩满归京<br>Farewell to Uncle Six, Who Has Finished His Tenure at Jen and Is Going Back to the Capital |
| 1123 | 鲁郡尧祠送吴五之琅琊<br>Seeing Off Wu Five to Ivory at Mound's Shrine in Lu |
| 1125 | 鲁郡尧祠送窦明府薄华还西京<br>Seeing Off Pohua Tou, a Magistrate, West to Capital at Mound's Shrine in Lu |
| 1130 | 金乡送韦八之西京<br>Seeing Off Wei Eight to Capital from Goldton |
| 1131 | 送薛九被谗去鲁<br>Seeing Off Slandered Hsüeh Nine to Lu |
| 1135 | 单父东楼秋夜送族弟沈之秦（时凝弟在席）<br>Seeing Off Shen, My Cousin, from Shanfu to Capital on an Autumn Night（Another Cousin, Ning, Is at the Feast） |

| | | |
|---|---|---|
| 1138 | 送族弟凝至晏堌单父三十里 | |
| | Accompanying My Cousin to Yanku, 15 Miles from Shanfu | |
| 1140 | 鲁城北郭曲腰桑下送张子还嵩阳 | |
| | Seeing Off Chang to Towershine at a Crooked Mulberry North of Luton | |
| 1143 | **古近体诗四十四首** | |
| | Old-new Rhythmic Poetry, 44 Poems | |
| 1145 | 送鲁郡刘长史迁弘农长史 | |
| | Seeing Off Liu, a Secretary in Lu to Be a Secretary in Great Farming | |
| 1148 | 送族弟单父主簿凝摄宋城主簿至郭南月桥却回栖霞山留饮赠之 | |
| | Seeing Off Ning, My Cousin, Secretary of Shanfu, to Be Secretary of Sung, Stopping South of Moon Bridge and Returning to Mt. Clouds for a Farewell Party | |
| 1150 | 鲁郡东石门送杜二甫 | |
| | Send-off of Fu Tu at Stone Gate, East Lu | |
| 1151 | 鲁郡尧祠送张十四游河北 | |
| | Seeing Off Chang Fourteen to Tour North of the River at Mound's Shrine in the County of Lu | |
| 1153 | 杭州送裴大泽赴庐州长史 | |
| | Seeing Off Tatse P'ei in Hangchow to His Secretary Post in Lodge | |
| 1154 | 灞陵行送别 | |
| | Farewell at Paridge Kiosk | |
| 1155 | 送贺监归四明应制 | |
| | Seeing Off Chihchang Ho to Mt. Four Bright, a Poem Composed by an Imperial Order | |
| 1157 | 送窦司马贬宜春 | |
| | Seeing Off Commander Tou Exiled to Fitspring | |
| 1159 | 送羽林陶将军 | |
| | To T'ao, General of Armed Escort | |
| 1160 | 送程刘二侍郎兼独孤判官赴安西幕府 | |
| | Seeing Off Ministers Ch'eng and Liu to Be Aides in Pacified West | |

Tent Office

1162 送侄良携二妓赴会稽，戏有此赠
Seeing Off Liang, My Nephew to Mt. Summit with Two Singers, a Poem for Fun

1163 送贺宾客归越
Seeing Off Chihchang Ho Back to Yüeh

1164 送张遥之寿阳幕府
Seeing Off Yao Chang to Lifeshine Tent Office

1166 送裴十八图南归嵩山二首
Seeing Off T'unan P'ei Back South to Mt. Tower, Two Poems

1170 同王昌龄送族弟襄归桂阳二首
Seeing Off My Cousin Hsiang Li Back to Cassiashine with Ch'angling Wang, Two Poems

1174 送外甥郑灌从军三首
Seeing Off My Nephew Kuan Cheng to Join the Army, Three Poems

1177 送于十八应四子举落第还嵩山
Seeing Off Yü Eighteen to Mt. Tower After He Failed Grand Test

1180 送别
Good-bye

1181 送族弟绾从军安西
Seeing Off My Cousin Kuan to Join the Army in Pacified West

1183 送梁公昌从信安北征
Seeing Off Ch'ang Liang to North Expedition Under Prince of Real Peace

1185 送白利从金吾董将军西征
Seeing Off Li Pai to the West Expedition Under General Tung of the Garrison

1187 送张秀才从军
Seeing Off Chang, a Showcharm, to Join the Army

1189 送崔度还吴度故人礼部员国辅之子
Seeing Off Tu Ts'ui Back to Wu, Who Is a Son of My Friend, Kuofu Ts'ui, a Councillor of the Ministry of Rites

| | | |
|---|---|---|
| 1191 | 送祝八之江东，赋得浣纱石 | |
| | Seeing Off Tsu Eight to the East, a Verse of Washing Stone | |
| 1193 | 送侯十一 | |
| | Seeing Off Hou Eleven | |
| 1195 | 鲁中送二从弟赴举之西京 | |
| | Seeing Off My Two Cousins to Capital to Take Grand Test | |
| 1197 | 奉饯高尊师如贵道士传道箓毕归北海 | |
| | Attending a Feast for Kao, a Wordist, to Return to North Sea After He Finishes Conducting a Wordist Conferment | |
| 1198 | 金陵送张十一再游东吴 | |
| | Seeing Off Chang Eleven to Tour East Wu Again | |
| 1200 | 送纪秀才游越 | |
| | Seeing Off Chi, a Showcharm, to Tour Yüeh | |
| 1202 | 送长沙陈太守二首 | |
| | Seeing Off Ch'en, Magistrate of Long Sand, Two Poems | |
| 1205 | 送杨燕之东鲁 | |
| | Seeing Off Yan Yang to East Lu | |
| 1207 | 送蔡山人 | |
| | Seeing Off Ts'ai, the Hermit | |
| 1209 | 送萧三十一之鲁中兼问稚子伯禽 | |
| | Seeing Off Hsiao Thirteen to Mid-Lu, Who May Go See My Son There | |
| 1211 | 送杨山人归嵩山 | |
| | Sending Off Yang, a Hermit, to Mt. Tower | |
| 1213 | 送殷淑三首 | |
| | Seeing Off Shu Yin, Three Poems | |
| 1216 | 送岑征君归鸣皋山 | |
| | Seeing Off Ts'en, a Recruit, to Mt. Chirping Bog | |
| 1219 | 送范山人归泰山 | |
| | Seeing Off Fan, the Hermit, Back to Mt. Arch | |

# 古近体诗三十四首
## Old-new Rhythmic Poetry, 34 Poems

## 秋日鲁郡尧祠亭上宴别杜补阙范侍御

我觉秋兴逸，
谁云秋兴悲？
山将落日去，
水与晴空宜。
鲁酒白玉壶，
送行驻金羁。
歇鞍憩古木，
解带挂横枝。
歌鼓川上亭，
曲度神飙吹。
云归碧海夕，
雁没青天时。
相失各万里，
茫然空尔思。

## A Farewell Party to Remonstrant Tu and Royal Servant Fan at Mound Shrine Kiosk in Lu on an Autumn Day

I think autumn can make one glad;
Who says autumn will make one sad?
The hills will take the sun away;
The brine and the blue calmly stay.
The jade pot filled with mellow wine,
Stop your horse for a drink, friend mine.
Rest your horse under the old tree;

Lay your sash on the twig near thee.

The song from the kiosk downstream flows;

The tune with the wind upward blows.

At dusk, mist and clouds merge on high;

The wild geese disappear in the sky.

Thousands of miles we are apart;

Blank sadness overloads my heart.

* jade pot: a pot usually alluding to the purity of the holder's heart and in some other cases alluding to the purity of the holder's heart.
* horse: a large solid-hoofed quadruped (*Equus caballus*) with coarse mane and tail, of various strains: Ferghana, Mongolian, Kazaks, Hequ, Karasahr and so on and of various colors: black, white, yellow, brown, dappled and so on, commonly in the domesticated state, employed as a beast of draught and burden and especially for riding upon.
* wild goose: an undomesticated goose that is caring and responsible, taken as a symbol of benevolence, righteousness, good manner, wisdom, and faith in Chinese culture.

## 别　鲁　颂

谁道泰山高，
下却鲁连节。
谁云秦军众，
摧却鲁连舌。
独立天地间，
清风洒兰雪。
夫子还倜傥，
攻文继前烈。
错落石上松，
无为秋霜折。
赠言镂宝刀，
千岁庶不灭。

## Goodbye to Sung Lu

Who says Mt. Arch there towers so high?
Compared with Lien Lu it's a short one.
Who says Ch'in's troops are ferocious?
They were thwarted by Lien Lu's tongue.
He stood between Heaven and earth,
Pure like wind, an orchid and snow.
You, my friend, so handsome and spruce,
After Lien Lu, ahead you go.
Rooted in deep rock, you're a pine,
Which in cold frost upright appears.
To you I give this word and sword,

Which will survive a thousand years.

* Mt. Arch: one of the Five Mountains in China, located in Shantung Province, along with Mt. Ever in Shanhsi, Mt. Scale in Hunan, Mt. Flora in Sha'anhsi, and Mt. Tower in Honan. Mt. Arch is the most sacred of the five, because 72 sovereigns in prehistoric China made sacrifices to the god of the mountain and 12 emperors made sacrifices from the Ch'in dynasty to the Ch'ing dynasty, clearly recorded in history books.
* Ch'in: the Ch'in State or the State of Ch'in (905 B.C.- 206 B.C.), enfeoffed as a dependency of Chough by King Piety of Chough in 905 B.C. and enfeoffed as a vassal state by King Peace of Chough in 770 B.C. In the ten years from 230 B.C. to 221 B.C., Ch'in wiped out the other six powers and became the first unified regime of China, i.e. the Ch'in Empire.
* orchid: a terrestrial or epiphytic monocotyledonous plant having thickened bulbous roots and often very showy distinctive flowers, one of the four most important floral images in Chinese literature, which are wintersweet, orchid, bamboo and chrysanthemum.
* Lien Lu: referring to Chunglien Lu (305 B.C.- 245 B.C.), a sophist from Ch'i in the late Spring and Autumn period. Once, the State of Ch'i lost a lot of soldiers when they tried to retake Liaoton. Lien Lu wrote a letter and launched it into the city. Persuaded by the letter, the commander in Liaoton committed suicide and left the city to Ch'i.

## 别中都明府兄

吾兄诗酒继陶君，  
试宰中都天下闻。  
东楼喜奉连枝会，  
南陌愁为落叶分。  
城隅渌水明秋日，  
海上青山隔暮云。  
取醉不辞留夜月，  
雁行中断惜离群。

## Farewell to Brother, Magistrate of Mid-town

Like Ch'ien T'ao you govern with verse and wine,
And your achievements are to the world known.
You hold a farewell feast called "Twigs Entwine";
I'll drift like a leaf in South, all alone.
The autumn water round the town gleams bright;
The dusky clouds shroud the sea mountains gray.
Let's drink and be drunk on this moonlit night;
Tomorrow from the flock I'll fly away.

\* Ch'ien T'ao: Poolbright T'ao (A.D. 352 – A.D. 427) or Yüanming T'ao if translated, a verse writer, poet, and litterateur in the Chin dynasty, and the founder of Chinese idyllism, who was once the magistrate of P'engtse.

## 梦游天姥吟留别

海客谈瀛洲,
烟涛微茫信难求。
越人语天姥,
云霞明灭或可睹。
天姥连天向天横,
势拔五岳掩赤城。
天台一万八千丈,
对此欲倒东南倾。
我欲因之梦吴越,
一夜飞度镜湖月。
湖月照我影,
送我至剡溪。
谢公宿处今尚在,
渌水荡漾清猿啼。
脚著谢公屐,
身登青云梯。
半壁见海日,
空中闻天鸡。
千岩万转路不定,
迷花倚石忽已暝。
熊咆龙吟殷岩泉,
栗深林兮惊层巅。
云青青兮欲雨,
水澹澹兮生烟。
列缺霹雳,
丘峦崩摧。
洞天石扉,

訇然中开。
青冥浩荡不见底，
日月照耀金银台。
霓为衣兮风为马，
云之君兮纷纷而来下。
虎鼓瑟兮鸾回车，
仙之人兮列如麻。
忽魂悸以魄动，
恍惊起而长嗟。
惟觉时之枕席，
失向来之烟霞。
世间行乐亦如此，
古来万事东流水。
别君去兮何时还？
且放白鹿青崖间，
须行即骑访名山。
安能摧眉折腰事权贵，
使我不得开心颜！

# My Dream of Mt. Sky Mum: To Go or Not to Go

Of Sea Shoal a hiker cackles:
All waves and haze, it's hard to see her trace.
Of Sky Mum a south folk babbles.
All clouds and rays, thereupon looms her face.
Mt. Sky Mum hits the sky and sweeps the sky,
Rising o'er Five Mounts and hiding Red Town.
Heaven Altar's eighteen thousand yards high;
Before Sky Mum, southeast it's falling down.

My dream leads me to Wu-and-Yüeh, South Land,
Where Mirror Lake accosts my moonlit dream.
The moon shines brightly on me and
Sees me all the way to the Shan Stream.
Today, Hsieh's residence is still o'er there,
Where blue water ripples and monkeys cry.
Hsieh's sandals so fitting I wear
And climb the ladder called Blue Sky.
The hillside sees at sea rise the sun
And thru the air hears roosters' crows.
Through rocks the trail's a meandering one,
Which traces blooms and crags till the dusk glows.
Bears roar, dragons caw and from rocks springs flow;
The woods shake, the peaks quake and none well stands.
It threatens rain tho the sky's blue;
Mist rises while water expands.
The thunders seem to clash;
The mountains seem to crash.
The cave shows its stone door
That opens with a roar.
The dark cave follows its endless brook course;
The sun and moon glisten o'er Silver Mound.
The rainbow is clothes and the wind a horse;
Fairies alighting from among clouds come around.
Tigers pluck the lute and rocs drive the cart,
And fairies there line up, what a large mass!
Taken my soul and shaken my heart,
I wake up to heave a sigh: alas!
Only my pillow and mat with me,
All gone off, nothing left, not the least.
All worldliness is like this, glee or spree;

Past and present like the River flow east.
Now leaving, I don't know when I can come back.
I just leave my white deer on the cliff now;
I'll ride it to the mountains when need be.
How can I to those lords and peers lower my brows and bow
So that I cannot laugh, happy and free?

* Mt. Sky Mum: a mountain located in Chechiang Province. It is said that one could hear immortals singing atop the mountain.
* Sea Shoal: one of the Three Fairy Islands on East Sea.
* Five Mounts: referring to the Five Mountains in China, including Mount Ever in Shanhsi, Mount Scale in Hunan, Mount Arch in Shantung, Mount Flora in Sha'anhsi, and Mount Tower in Honan, which symbolizes the unity of the Chinese nation from north, south, east, west and central part.
* Red Town: a mountain in Chechiang Province.
* Heaven Altar: a mountain in Chechiang Province.
* Wu-and-Yüeh: an area covering present-day Chiangsu, Shanghai, Chechiang, Anhui, and Chianghsi.
* Mirror Lake: a lake located in the south of Shaohsing, Chechiang.
* the Shan Stream: a main stream with rich cultural attractions in present-day Shengchow, Chechiang Province.
* Hsieh: referring to Lingyün Hsieh (A.D. 385 – A.D. 433), a highborn poet, Buddhist and traveler, famous for landscape poetry. He invented a pair of sandals that are ideal for climbing mountains.
* rooster: the male of the chicken that struts with pride and crows at dawn.
* dragon: a fabulous serpent-like giant winged animal that can change its girth and length, a symbol of benevolence and sovereignty in Chinese culture.

## 留别曹南群官之江南

我昔钓白龙,
放龙溪水傍。
道成本欲去,
挥手凌苍苍。
时来不关人,
谈笑游轩皇。
献纳少成事,
归休辞建章。
十年罢西笑,
览镜如秋霜。
闭剑琉璃匣,
炼丹紫翠房。
身佩豁落图,
腰垂虎鞶囊。
仙人驾彩凤,
志在穷遐荒。
恋子四五人,
裴回未翱翔。
东流送白日,
骤歌兰蕙芳。
仙宫两无从,
人间久摧藏。
范蠡说句践,
屈平去怀王。
飘飘紫霞心,
流浪忆江乡。
愁为万里别,

复此一衔觞。
淮水帝王州,
金陵绕丹阳。
楼台照海色,
衣马摇川光。
及此北望君,
相思泪成行。
朝云落梦渚,
瑶草空高堂。
帝子隔洞庭,
青枫满潇湘。
怀君路绵邈,
览古情凄凉。
登岳眺百川,
杳然万恨长。
知恋峨眉去,
弄景偶骑羊。

# Going South, Farewell to the Officials in Ts'aonan

I caught a white dragon before
And laid it o'er there, the stream by.
The Word attained, I would high soar,
Waving my hand to the blue sky.
To the world I'll no longer heed;
With Cartshaft I can laugh and play.
My pleas and plans seldom succeed;
From Letters Hall I'll go away.
It's ten years now since I came west;

My gray hair shows in the mirror.
My sword is now laid in the chest;
I work the forge for elixir.
I wear an Intricate Word Sign
And a tiger skin on my waist.
I'll ride a phoenix with mate mine
To cruise the wild, a vast land waste.
But four or five friends, I love you,
And feel it hard to fly away.
Each day the Yellow does there flow,
And songs with orchid balm there stay.
The fairy castle's there for me,
Alluring those in the world wild.
Li Fan to Kouchien made a plea;
Yüan Chü was by King Huai exiled.
Blown, blown, my purple-cloud-like heart,
I miss my home, a river town!
For ten thousand miles I'll depart;
Let me drink to my sadness drown.
The Huai River round Gold Hill glows;
Gold Hill does encircle Red Sun.
The tower tilts to greet the sea hues;
Carts and arrays are by waves shone.
Here I turn north to look for you;
For you two strings of my tears fall.
In my dream ashore is dawn hue;
Magic grass waves in the broad hall.
By Lake Cavehall, we're kept apart;
To the Hsiang River maples sough.
The long way does sadden my heart,
The old sites are bleak, bleak enow.

Uphill all the streams I espy;
My grief so long downstream does float,
I'm yearning to climb up Mt. Brow
And go to Bliss, riding a goat.

* White Dragon: Sir Glare, fond of fishing, once caught a white dragon. He felt scared and released it. Later, Glare got a white fish with a prescription in its body. He found all the ingredients and took them as elixir. Three years later, the white dragon came to pick him up onto a hill.
* the Word: referring to Tao if transliterated, the most significant and profoundest concept in Chinese philosophy. The Word is fully elucidated in *The Word and the World*, the single book that Laocius wrote all his wisdom into. Its importance can be seen in this verse: "The Word is void, but its use is infinite. O deep! It seems to be the root of all things."
* Cartshaft: alias Lord Yellow, the first of the five heavenly gods in myth and the earliest ancestor of Chinese.
* Letters Hall: a palace of the Han dynasty, implying the court.
* Intricate Word Sign: referring to Wordist costumes.
* a tiger skin: a sachet for Wordists.
* the Yellow: referring to the Yellow River.
* Li Fan: Li Fan (536 B.C.- 448 B.C.), a politician, militarist, economist and Wordist in later years of the Spring and Autumn Period, who helped Kouchien, the king of Wu restore his country.
* Kouchien: Kouchien (520 B.C.- 465 B.C.), King of Yüeh, successfully wiped out the State of Wu for revenge, and burnt Wu's Palace around 473 B.C.
* Yüan Ch'ü: Yüan Ch'ü (340 B.C.- 278 B.C.), a great patriotic poet and official of Ch'u, who threw himself into the river, so aggrieved at his broken state.
* King Huai: King Huai of Ch'u (355 B.C.- 296 B.C.), who rejected Yüan Ch'ü's proposal and as a result died in captivity in Ch'in.
* the Huai River: one of the seven rivers in China, between the Long River and the Yellow River, 1,000 kilometers long.
* Gold Hill: referring to Nanking, one of the most well-known ancient capitals in China.
* Red Sun: referring to Tanyang if transliterated, present-day Junchow District, Chenchiang, Chiangsu Province.
* Cavehall: a large lake in today's Hunan Province.
* maple: any of a large genus (*Acer*) of deciduous trees of the north temperate zone,

with opposite leaves that turn red in autumn and a fruit of two joined samaras, a symbol of cordial love and good luck because of its bright fiery color.
* Mt. Brow: one of the four Buddhist mountains, located in Ssuch'uan Province, named for its elegant brow-shaped silhouette viewed from a distance.
* goat: a hollow-horned ruminant (genus *Capra*) of rocky and mountainous regions, related to the sheep and including wild and domesticated forms.

## 留别于十一兄逖裴十三游塞垣

太公渭川水，
李斯上蔡门。
钓周猎秦安黎元，
小鱼兔何足言。
天张云卷有时节，
吾徒莫叹羝触藩。
于公白首大梁野，
使人怅望何可论。
既知朱亥为壮士，
且愿束心秋毫里。
秦赵虎争血中原，
当去抱关救公子。
裴生览千古，
龙鸾炳文章。
悲吟雨雪动林木，
放书辍剑思高堂。
劝尔一杯酒，
拂尔裘上霜。
尔为我楚舞，
吾为尔楚歌。
且探虎穴向沙漠，
鸣鞭走马凌黄河。
耻作易水别，
临歧泪滂沱。

# Farewell to Brother Yü Eleven and P'ei Thirteen at the Great Wall

Great Grand fished by the river Wei;
Ssu Li hunted out of Tsai Gate.
Fishing or hunting, folks' pains they'd allay;
How could minnows and hares be seen as great?
It's been arranged that clouds roll or are rolled;
Don't you sigh that entrapped I am, a sheep.
Mister Yü's a gray haired recluse, so old;
How can we comment on him but there peep?
Hai Chu was a brave gallant as we know;
He would bury himself in books, so grave.
Ch'in and Chao struggled and caused blood to flow;
I wish I had gone there to Crown Prince save.
Mr. P'ei, you've verse present and past,
And your own works like plumage shine.
I sigh the flurry would the forest blast;
My books and sword doffed, I miss parents mine.
Do drink a cup of wine I pray
While I dust frost off your array.
For me you dance a Ch'u dance;
For you I sing a Ch'u trance.
I'll go to the desert to hit the den;
I'll cross the River and run to the glen.
I'm ashamed of a sad good-bye;
I'm abashed at a rain-like cry.

* the Great Wall: usually called Ten-thousand-li Great Wall, a giant project undertaken

in different periods of Chinese history to defend China from northern nomadic invasions, mostly first built in the Ch'in dynasty, third century B.C., by forced labour including political prisoners.
* Great Grand: an influential strategist and statesman. Though he was a butcher at his young age, Great Grand remained diligent in hardship, expecting to display his ability for the country one day, but he did not make any achievement before he was 70 years old. He went west at the age of 72, fishing as he waited for King Civil, and finally won his appreciation.
* Ssu Li: Ssu Li (284 B.C. - 208 B.C.), a renowned statesman, litterateur and calligrapher, whose political ideas have had a profound impact on China and laid the foundation of China's political system for more than two thousand years. Before he went to Ch'in, Li was a hunter in hometown, Tsai Gate.
* minnows and hares: minnows are small fish and hares are rodents, proverbial for their timidity, so they are regarded as something insignificant.
* sheep: a medium-sized domesticated ruminant of the genus *Ovis*, highly prized for its flesh, wool and skin, regarded as meek and mild, a symbol of beauty and purity, used as a sacrifice in both Western and Eastern cultures.
* Mister Yü: referring to Yü Eleven.
* Hai Chu: a butcher who was treated with great courtesy by Faithridge, a prince of Way, and became his hanger-on. When the State of Chao was attacked by a hostile state and its capital Hantan was beleaguered, Hsin-ling and Chu Hai went to the rescue. Hai Chu, a very strong man, brained an irresolute general with a heavy hammer, while, by taking command of his army, Faithridge raised the siege of Hantan.
* Mr. Pei: referring to Pei Thirteen.

# 留别王司马嵩

鲁连卖谈笑,
岂是顾千金。
陶朱虽相越,
本有五湖心。
余亦南阳子,
时为梁甫吟。
苍山容偃蹇,
白日惜颓侵。
愿一佐明主,
功成还旧林。
西来何所为,
孤剑托知音。
鸟爱碧山远,
鱼游沧海深。
呼鹰过上蔡,
卖畚向嵩岑。
他日闲相访,
丘中有素琴。

## Farewell to Commander Sung Wang

Chunglien Lu his talks and laughs sold;
Did he talk and laugh for much gold?
Li Fan from Yüeh premier became;
To be a recluse was his aim.
I just want to follow Great Glare,

*Ode to Liang* is my cherished air.
The hills draw me from the vain fad;
But the setting sun makes me sad.
I wish I helped a Lord divine
Before I go to the woods fine.
Why do I come here to the west?
Because here I have my friend best.
Birds in remote hills freely coo;
Fish swim deeply in oceans blue.
I call eagles 'cross Ts'ai to fly,
And sell dustpans for Mt. Tower high.
If you come to see me someday,
In the woods the lute we can play.

* Chunglien Lu: Chunglien Lu (cir. A.D. 305 – A.D. 245), a political strategist, a sophist. He once helped Lord Plain of Chao successfully persuade the State of Way to fight together against Ch'in. After that, he declined the awards given by Lord Plain and went away.
* Li Fan: Li Fan (536 B.C.– 448 B.C.), a renowned statesman, strategist, economist and Wordist in the Spring and Autumn period. Fan changed his name to live in seclusion after he helped the State of Yüeh wipe out Wu.
* Great Glare: referring to Bright Chuke (A.D. 181 – A.D. 234), a statesman and strategist, the prime minister of the Kingdom of Shu in the period of the Three Kingdoms (A.D. 220 – A.D. 265).
* *Ode to Liang*: a verse that frequently chanted by Great Glare.
* eagle: a diurnal bird of prey of the family Accipitridae of worldwide distribution, notable for keen sight and strong flight, usually trained as a hunter and praised as a hero in Chinese culture.
* Ts'ai: referring to Ts'ai Gate, the hometown of Ssu Li.
* sell dustpan: In the Eastern Chin dynasty, Meng Wang (A.D. 325 – A.D. 375) lived by selling dustpans but was keen on military strategy. He became a prime minister and grand general by virtue of his talent and ambition.
* Mt. Tower: located in the west of present-day Honan Province, one of the Five Mountains in Chinese culture.

# 夜 别 张 五

吾多张公子，  
别酌酬高堂。  
听歌舞银烛，  
把酒轻罗裳。  
横笛弄秋月，  
琵琶弹陌桑。  
龙泉解锦带，  
为尔倾千觞。

# Farewell to Chang Five at Night

Mister Chang so much I adore;  
Let's drink to our farewell, drink more.  
The song allures the candle bright;  
The wine does our array delight.  
The flute does the autumn moon play;  
The lute does the mulberries sway.  
For you my sword lash I untie  
And cup by cup we drink till high.

* candle: a cylinder of tallow, wax, or other solid fat, containing a wick, to give light when burning, first seen in literature in the Eastern Han dynasty. The most famous lines about candles are from a poem by a T'ang poet named Shangyin Li, "Silkworms stop offering silk when they die; / Candles become ash as their tears run dry."
* The lute does the mulberries sway: an allusion to *Mulberries on the Lane*, a Han conservatoire poem.

* mulberry: the edible, berry-like fruit of a tree (genus *Morus*) whose leaves are valued for silkworm culture, and the tree itself, first cultivated in the drainage area of the Yellow River in China about five thousand years ago.

## 魏郡别苏明府因北游

魏都接燕赵,
美女夸芙蓉。
淇水流碧玉,
舟车日奔冲。
青楼夹两岸,
万室喧歌钟。
天下称豪贵,
游此每相逢。
洛阳苏季子,
剑戟森词锋。
六印虽未佩,
轩车若飞龙。
黄金数百镒,
白璧有几双。
散尽空掉臂,
高歌赋还邛。
落魄乃如此,
何人不相从?
远别隔两河,
云山杳千重。
何时更杯酒,
再得论心胸。

## Farewell to Magistrate Su at Way's Capital to Tour North

Way's capital's close to Yan-Chao,
Where girls like lotus blossoms blush.
The Ch'i River flows on, so blue,
Where day and night boats and skiffs rush.
Blue brothels line up on both banks;
Strings and songs fill the rooms with cheer.
It's a place for rich men and peers;
Sometimes gallants you can meet here.
You're like Sir Chi Su in Loshine,
A good swordsman, a talent smart.
Tho you're not premier of six states,
Like a flying dragon runs your cart.
I have a hundred bars of gold,
And white jade, I have a few pairs.
I squander them all, all away,
And singing, go home in high airs.
I'm like this e'en in a poor state;
Who will not follow his free will?
By two rivers we'll be kept off,
Cloud in cloud and hill upon hill.
When can we meet and drink a cup,
Laughing, talking and cheering up?

\* the Ch'i River: an ancient affluent of the Yellow River.
\* skiff: a light rowboat for fishing or lotus-picking and so on; formerly a sailing vessel.
\* Sir Chi Su: referring to Ch'in Su (? - 284 B.C.), a renowned strategist, diplomat in

the Warring States period.
* Loshine: Loyang if transliterated, one of the four ancient capitals in China, along with Long Peace (Hsi'an), Gold Hill (Nanking) and Peking, and it was the second largest city in the T'ang dynasty.
* dragon: Though variously understood as a large reptile, a marine monster, a jackal and so on in Western culture, it has been esteemed as a fabulous serpent-like giant winged animal, a totem of the Chinese nation and a symbol of benevolence and sovereignty in Chinese culture.

# 留别西河刘少府

秋发已种种,
所为竟无成。
闲倾鲁壶酒,
笑对刘公荣。
谓我是方朔,
人间落岁星。
白衣千万乘,
何事去天庭。
君亦不得意,
高歌羡鸿冥。
世人若醯鸡,
安可识梅生。
虽为刀笔吏,
缅怀在赤城。
余亦如流萍,
随波乐休明。
自有两少妾,
双骑骏马行。
东山春酒绿,
归隐谢浮名。

## Farewell to Sheriff Liu of Westriver

Accomplishments I have made not
But that my hair's grown gray and thin.
Now free, I pour wine from the pot

And to Liu, the sheriff, I grin.
You say I'm a hermit downtown
Like Jupiter as does from high fall.
In white clothes I can help the crown;
Why should I go to Heaven Hall?
Reduced, you have no mood to preen,
Singing to the swans in the blue.
The worldly peoples are gnats mean;
You are a sage, how do they know?
Tho you have no high rank to lead,
You wish to live there in Red Town.
And I am just like a duckweed,
Following the waves up and down.
Charming concubines I have twain,
Who ride horses alongside me.
Why should I care about fame vain?
Drink wine in the East Hills, so free.

* Red Town: Mt. Red Town, a mountain in Chechiang Province.
* concubine: a cohabitant or secondary wife. China was a polygamous society from prehistoric years till the first half of the twentieth century. An ordinary man could have three wives and four concubines and a concubine could be bartered or sold or given as a gift in ancient China. An emperor might have thousands of concubines, for example, Emperor Deepsire had 40,000.
* Jupiter: the fifth planet from the sun, around which it revolves about 12 years at a mean distance of 483,000,000 miles.
* swan: a large web-footed, long-necked bird (subfamily *Cygninae*), allied to but heavier than the goose and noted for its grace on the water, as the whooper, the trumpeter swan, and the whistling swan.
* gnat: any of various small dipterous flies with long, many-jointed antennae, as the buffalo gnat, punkies and midges.
* the East Hills: a place for reclusion, located in today's Shaohsing, Chechiang Province, the hills where An Hsieh (A.D. 320 – A.D. 385), a statesman and litterateur

with high reputation, lived with ease and kept declining official positions until he was in his forties. It is often used as a metaphor for reclusion.
* duckweed: any of several small, disk-shaped, floating aquatic plants common in streams and ponds.

## 颍阳别元丹丘之淮阳

吾将元夫子,
异姓为天伦。
本无轩裳契,
素以烟霞亲。
尝恨迫世网,
铭意俱未伸。
松柏虽寒苦,
羞逐桃李春。
悠悠市朝间,
玉颜日缁磷。
所失重山岳,
所得轻埃尘。
精魄渐芜秽,
衰老相凭因。
我有锦囊诀,
可以持君身。
当餐黄金药,
去为紫阳宾。
万事难并立,
百年犹崇晨。
别尔东南去,
悠悠多悲辛。
前志庶不易,
远途期所遵。
已矣归去来,
白云飞天津。

## Farewell to Redknoll Yüan, Who's Leaving for Huaishine from Yingshine

O Redknoll, my teacher, my friend,
You're like my sibling I hold dear.
High ranks are not my aim or end;
To misty scenes I would get near.
The world is such a net I hate;
I have not reached my intense aim.
Tho hard and cold, the pine is great;
To chase vainglory is its shame.
In Vanity Fair all's thrown and tossed;
Good complexion is by dirt stained.
Like a mound is what I have lost;
Like a midge is what I have gained.
As one's mood is low, he grows slack,
And signs of age on his face creep.
Recently, I have learned a knack,
With which you can good health keep.
On gold elixir you should dine,
So to join Purpleshine the sage.
No two things can both suit you fine;
A hundred years hastes off the stage.
I'll go southeast now we're apart;
My sadness will heavily weigh.
But I will never change my heart;
No matter how, I will fast stay.
Whatever comes on will go by,
Like clouds that o'er Heaven Ford fly.

* Redknoll Yüan: a adept Wordist and an important friend of Pai Li's. Pai Li met him at the age of twenty and once lived in seclusion with him on Mt. Tower. With their twenty-four years' friendship and correspondence, Rendknoll exerted great influence on Pai Li, who wrote 14 poems dedicated to the former.
* Vanity Fair: the vulgar dust world characterized by folly and frivolity.
* midge: any of various families of small, two-winged, gnatlike dipteran insects, including the gall midges and biting midges.
* elixir: a hypothetical substance sought by medical alchemists to change base metals into gold or prolong life indefinitely.
* Purpleshine: an immortal in Chinese mythology.

## 留别广陵诸公

忆昔作少年,
结交赵与燕。
金羁络骏马,
锦带横龙泉。
寸心无疑事,
所向非徒然。
晚节觉此疏,
猎精草太玄。
空名束壮士,
薄俗弃高贤。
中回圣明顾,
挥翰凌云烟。
骑虎不敢下,
攀龙忽堕天。
还家守清真,
孤洁励秋蝉。
炼丹费火石,
采药穷山川。
卧海不关人,
租税辽东田。
乘兴忽复起,
棹歌溪中船。
临醉谢葛强,
山公欲倒鞭。
狂歌自此别,
垂钓沧浪前。

# A Poem for Friends in Broadridge

When I was young, as I recall,
Gallant friends from north I made.
Our steeds in gold bridles charmed all;
I wore a Spring Sword and brocade.
We'd no worries and were so bold,
Happy with whate'er we would do.
Such crudeness I realized when old,
And delved into the deep and true.
Vain fame entraps a gallant ace;
World dust detracts a savant high.
Middle-aged, I had the Lord's grace;
My verse would soar up to the sky.
One's hard on a tiger astride;
A crane rider falls from the blue.
Back home, I would by truth abide,
Like a cicada singing: True.
For elixir I've burned much stone;
To pick herbs all hills I'd explore.
By the seaside I lived alone,
And farmed on this land of East Liao.
With such a spur I rose again;
A song I sang, the oar I plied.
Feeling drunk, I thanked Hillman's man,
And lay drunk with Hillman beside.
Singing aloud I'd from here go
And fish at sea, on the waves blue.

* Broadridge: an alternative name for Yangchow, an important city in today's Chiangsu Province, the greatest canal port in China and the centre of luxury trades in the T'ang dynasty.
* Spring Sword: a legendary sword made by Yehtzu Ou, a renowned swordsmith.
* on a tiger: referring to Newmoon East (154 B.C.- 93 B.C.), a jocular and witted official serving Lord Martial of Han, rode a tiger to travel around.
* cicada: a homopterous insect that sings its song of summer and shrills in autumn, a symbol of death and resurrection in Chinese culture because of its metamorphosis and recycle. Therefore, in ancient China, a jade cicada figure was put in the mouth of a dead body with such an intention of eternal life.
* elixir: a hypothetical substance sought by medical alchemists to change base metals into gold or prolong life indefinitely.
* East Liao: an area east of the Liao River and north of East Sea, about 500 square kilometers.
* Hillman: Chien Shan (A.D. 253 - A.D. 312), a celebrity and general in the Chin dynasty, the fifth son of T'ao Shan, one of the Seven Sages of the Bamboo Grove in the Chin dynasty. He was gentle and graceful as his father. When he was an official, the nation was falling apart and other officials were worried and depressed. Hillman, however, lived a casual life. Every time he hanged out, he would hold a banquet and get drunk at the High Sun Pool.

# 广 陵 赠 别

玉瓶沽美酒，
数里送君还。
系马垂杨下，
衔杯大道间。
天边看渌水，
海上见青山。
兴罢各分袂，
何须醉别颜。

# Farewell to Broadridge

Taking a pot with wine inside,
You have followed me many miles.
Our horses to the willows tied,
Our drinking the broad way beguiles.
I see water merge with the sky
And green hills on the sea appear.
After this drink we'll say good bye,
Don't look at me drunk without cheer.

* Broadridge: an alternative name for Yangchow.
* willow: any of a large genus of shrubs and trees related to the poplars, having generally narrow leaves, smooth branches, and often long, slender, pliant, and sometimes pendent branchlets, a symbol of farewell or nostalgia in Chinese culture. The best image is in *Vetch We Pick*, a verse in *The Book of Songs*, which reads like this: When we left long ago, / The willows waved adieu. / Now back to our home town, / We meet snow falling down.

# 感时留别从兄徐王延年从弟延陵

天籁何参差,
噫然大块吹。
玄元包橐籥,
紫气何逶迤。
七叶运皇化,
千龄光本支。
仙风生指树,
大雅歌螽斯。
诸王若鸾虬,
肃穆列藩维。
哲兄锡茅土,
圣代罗荣滋。
九卿领徐方,
七步继陈思。
伊昔全盛日,
雄豪动京师。
冠剑朝凤阙,
楼船侍龙池。
鼓钟出朱邸,
金翠照丹墀。
君王一顾盼,
选色献蛾眉。
列戟十八年,
未曾辄迁移。
大臣小喑呜,
谪窜天南垂。
长沙不足舞,

贝锦且成诗。
佐郡浙江西,
病闲绝驱驰。
阶轩日苔藓,
鸟雀噪檐帷。
时乘平肩舆,
出入畏人知。
北宅聊偃憩,
欢愉恤茕嫠。
羞言梁苑地,
烜赫耀旌旗。
兄弟八九人,
吴秦各分离。
大贤达机兆,
岂独虑安危。
小子谢麟阁,
雁行忝肩随。
令弟字延陵,
凤毛出天姿。
清英神仙骨,
芬馥茝兰蕤。
梦得春草句,
将非惠连谁?
深心紫河车,
与我特相宜。
金膏犹罔象,
玉液尚磷缁。
伏枕寄宾馆,
宛同清漳湄。
药物多见馈,
珍羞亦兼之。

谁道溟渤深，
犹言浅恩慈。
鸣蝉游子意，
促织念归期。
骄阳何太赫，
海水烁龙龟。
百川尽凋枯，
舟楫阁中逵。
策马摇凉月，
通宵出郊歧。
泣别目眷眷，
伤心步迟迟。
愿言保明德，
王室仁清夷。
搀袂何所道？
援毫投此辞。

# Farewell to My Cousins, Yannien, Lord of Hsu, and Track Hills

The Heaven does sound high and low,
And all over the earth does blow.
All is by Heaven and earth blessed
And Laocius in great bliss went west.
Seven Lords have succeeded Crown;
Thousands of reigns will carry on.
Blessed air generates from great trees;
*Katydids* is sung to a breeze.
All lords like phoenixes at court
Our nation and Heaven support.

You have been granted fertile earth,
So all your trees lush leaves put forth.
A grandee, you rule the Hsu State;
Like Chih you write verse fast and great.
When King of Hsu ruled, his best days,
His greatness did the court amaze.
In full array you worship Lord
And in the pool serve Him aboard.
Bells and drums boost the court, behold
And the red steps are touched with gold.
His Majesty looks back to smile,
And the chosen belles Him beguile.
Eighteen years you've guarded the crown;
Ne'er have you moved out of the town.
Now the courtier does you resent;
South into exile you are sent.
Your won't be fulfilled in Long Sand;
You write verse on a brocade grand.
An aide's post you hold in Hangchow;
On sick leave, to ride you won't go.
Upon the steps green moss does grow;
On the eaves some birds chirp and crow.
Your sedan cart made low and slow,
You won't disturb folks on the go.
In North Residence you just rest;
The widows are calmed, not depressed.
Mentioning your Old House you're shy;
Then all flags to the sun flew high.
Eight or nine brothers now from home
Depart and in Wu or Ch'in roam.
A sage's gain or loss is designed;

How could one his own danger mind?
I feel honored to be with you
And follow you up where you go.
Our younger brother called Tract Hills
Is a phoenix with golden frills.
He looks handsome with divine charm
And like an orchid sending balm.
In your dream comes a superb line;
If not Hui Lien, who could so shine?
He loves his Purple River Cart;
We know each other heart to heart.
Elixir has not yet been gained;
Nectar has been by the world stained.
Ill, in the hotel I repose,
Like the limpid Chang River flows.
Thank you for medicine so good
Together with lots of best food.
Who says so deep is the ocean?
Not as deep as your emotion!
Cicadas know how deep you feel;
Crickets yearn for you a great deal.
How hot the flaming sun does turn!
The sea water will turtles burn!
All rivers dry, water no more;
Aground are all craft, boat and oar.
The moon so cool, our horses neigh,
All night in the suburb we play.
When it comes for us to depart,
We feel so sad, laden each heart.
For His Majesty's grace I pray
So the royals can peaceful stay.

> What can I say, holding your sleeve?
> I write you this verse while I leave.

* Laocius: one of the most influential philosophers of Wordism in China, the proponent of quietism. Laocius wrote all his wisdom into a single book of about five thousand words, which came to be known as *The World and the World*.
* *Katydids*: a poem in *The Book of Songs*, a stanza of which reads like this: Katydids take wings / And gather along. / May you have offsprings / As a large throng.
* Phoenix: In Chinese myths, phoenixes, auspicious birds, unlike ordinary ones, only perch on parasol trees, and only eat bamboo shoots and pearly stone.
* Chih: referring to Chih Ts'ao (A.D. 192 – A.D. 232), a renowned litterateur in the Three Kingdoms period. He once completed a poem within seven steps.
* red steps: the steps, painted in red, leading up to an imperial palace or an official or monastic hall, frequently occurring in classic Chinese literature.
* Long Sand: referring to Ch'angsha if transliterated, the capital city of present-day Hunan Province.
* Hangchow: the capital of present-day Chechiang Province.
* Purple River Cart: a term in Chinese alchemy. Since the T'ang dynasty, there have been two explanations of Purple River Cart: first, it refers to kidneys; secondly, vapour that circulates endlessly.
* elixir: a hypothetical substance sought by medical alchemists to change base metals into gold or prolong life indefinitely.
* nectar: in Chinese and Greek mythologies, the drink of the gods or fairies, and in botany, the saccharine substance secreted by some plants and forming the base of natural honey.
* cicada: a homopterous insect that sings its song of summer and shrills in autumn, a symbol of death and resurrection in Chinese culture because of its metamorphosis and recycle. Therefore, in ancient China, a jade cicada figure was put in the mouth of a dead body with such an intention of eternal life.
* cricket: a leaping orthopterous insect, with long antennae and three segments in each tarsus, the male of which makes a chirping sound by friction of forewings, a common image of a quiet night in Chinese literature.

## 别储邕之剡中

借问剡中道，
东南指越乡。
舟从广陵去，
水入会稽长。
竹色溪下绿，
荷花镜里香。
辞君向天姥，
拂石卧秋霜。

## Leaving for Shan, Farewell to Yung Ch'u

"The way to Shan, may I ask you?"
"Southeast to Yüeh Land you may go."
The boat from Broadbridge starts to row;
The water to Summit does flow.
The bamboo greens the flowing stream;
The lotus flowers so mirrored gleam.
Leaving you, to Sky Mum I go;
Stroking stone, I'll lie on frost hue.

* Shan: referring to the Shan Stream, a main stream with rich cultural attractions in present-day Shengchow, Chechiang Province.
* Broadridge: an alternative name for Yangchow.
* Summit: referring to Mt. Summit, the K'uaichi Mountains in present-day Chechiang Province, where Worm convened a summit attended by vassal lords, hence the name.
* bamboo: a tall, tree-like or shrubby grass in tropical and semi-tropical regions, a symbol of integrity and altitude, one of the four most important images in Chinese

literature, which are wintersweet, orchid, bamboo and chrysanthemum. Plankbridge Cheng (A.D. 1693 – A.D. 1765), A Ching poet, speaks of its character in a poem Bamboo Rooted in the Rock: "You bite the green hill and ne'er rest. / Roots in the broken crag, you grow, / And stand erect although hard pressed. / East, west, south, north, let the wind blow."

* lotus: one of the various plants of the waterlily family, characterized by their large floating round leaves and showy flowers, especially the white or pink Asian lotus, used as a religious symbol in Hinduism and Buddhism. In Chinese culture, it is a symbol of purity and elegance, unsoiled though out of soil, so clean with all leaves green, is a common image in Chinese literature, as two lines of a lyric by Hsiu Ouyang (A.D. 1007 –A.D. 1072) read: "A thunder brings rain to the wood and pool, / The rain hushes the lotus, drips cool."

* Sky Mum: Mt. Sky Mum, a mountain located in Chechiang Province. It is said that one could hear immortals singing up on the mountain.

## 留别金陵诸公

海水昔飞动,
三龙纷战争。
钟山危波澜,
倾侧骇奔鲸。
黄旗一扫荡,
割壤开吴京。
六代更霸王,
遗迹见都城。
至今秦淮间,
礼乐秀群英。
地扇邹鲁学,
诗腾颜谢名。
五月金陵西,
祖余白下亭。
欲寻庐峰顶,
先绕汉水行。
香炉紫烟灭,
瀑布落太清。
若攀星辰去,
挥手缅含情。

## A Poem for My Friends in Gold Hill

The sea surged and bellowed to roar;
Three dragons fought to win the war.
The Bell Hills were drowned, peaks and dales,

And rushed down all the way like whales.
The yellow flags waved up and down,
Hence appeared Wu's capital town.
Here six dynasties there have been;
The ruins of their power can be seen.
On both banks of the Ch'in-Huai there,
Rites, music, talents, belles, all flare.
Scholars and poets also arrive;
Yan's flair and Hsiehs' sparkles all thrive.
West of the Gold Hill in late May,
At White Kiosk a feast tune we play.
I will go and climb Mt. Lodge high
And the Han River I'll walk by.
Mt. Censer gives off purple smoke,
Which may the cataract well choke.
Atop the peak I'd climb stars higher;
To you I wave, eyes sending fire.

* Gold Hill: referring to Nanking, one of the most well-known ancient capitals in China.
* Three dragons: indicating the Three Kingdoms.
* dragon: a fabulous serpent-like giant winged animal that can change its girth and length, a symbol of benevolence and sovereignty in Chinese culture.
* the Bell Hills: hills in Gold Hill.
* yellow flags: army flags, used for troops led by a commander.
* Yan: referring to Yanchih Yan (A.D. 384 – A.D. 456), a litterateur in the Southern Dynasties period, as famous as Lingyün Hsieh.
* Hsieh: referring to Lingyün Hsieh (A.D. 385 – A.D. 433), a highborn poet, Buddhist and traveler in the Southern Dynasties period, famous for landscape poems. He invented a pair of sandals that are ideal for climbing mountains.
* Mt. Lodge: a famous mountain with historic, cultural and religious attractions, located in present-day Chianghsi Province.
* the Han River: the longest branch of the Long River, having an important position in Chinese history.
* Mt. Censer: a scenic peak of Mt. Lodge, looking like an incense burner.

## 口　号

食出野田美，
酒临远水倾。
东流若未尽，
应见别离情。

## An Oral Impromptu

From better fields comes better food;
From distant water, good wine's brewed.
The river flows east without end,
The parting grief will its heart rend.

## 金陵酒肆留别

风吹柳花满店香,
吴姬压酒唤客尝。
金陵子弟来相送,
欲行不行各尽觞。
请君试问东流水,
别意与之谁短长?

## Farewell in a Wine Shop in Gold Hill

All o'er the inn wind blows catkins to fly;
The Wu girl offers me a cup to try.
My friends in Gold Hill all come for good bye;
We'd part but can't part, just drink our cup dry.
East flowing water, may I ask you why?
Why is your flow not longer than my sigh?

* Gold Hill: referring to Nanking, one of the most well-known ancient capitals in China. This city has had more than twenty names such as Forgeton, Fodder Ridge, Buildgain, River Peace and so on since the Spring and Autumn period.
* catkin: a deciduous scaly spike of flowers, as in the willow, an image of helpless drifting or wandering in Chinese literature.

## 金陵白下亭留别

驿亭三杨树，
正当白下门。
吴烟暝长条，
汉水啮古根。
向来送行处，
回首阻笑言。
别后若见之，
为余一攀翻。

## Farewell at White Bower in Gold Hill

The post kiosk has three willow trees,
Which the entrance of White Kiosk sees.
Their long twigs and boughs the mist veils;
Their olden roots the water fails.
My friends come on to say adieu;
Their bitter smiles face this sad view.
If you see them when we're apart,
Please send a sallow to my heart.

* White Bower: a post not far from East Gate of Gold Hill, that is, today's Nanking.
* Gold Hill: referring to Nanking, one of the most well-known ancient cities in China, a strategic fort as a gateway to the sea, which has been the capital of Wu, Chin, and many other states or kingdoms, such as the six empires called Six Dynasties and has flourished immensely with increasing trade and travel.

## 别东林寺僧

东林送客处，
月出白猿啼。
笑别庐山远，
何烦过虎溪。

## Farewell to the Monk at East Wood Temple

At East Wood you wave me good bye;
The moon out, the white monkeys cry.
To my monk friend I brightly beam:
"Don't go beyond the Tiger Stream."

* East Wood: a temple. East Wood Temple, built in A.D. 384, is one of the oldest temples on Mt. Lodge.
* monkey: any of a group of primates usually having a flat, hairless face, elongate limbs, hands and feet adapted for grasping, and a highly developed nervous system, including marmosets, baboons, and macaques, but not the anthropoid apes, though monkeys and apes are used alternatively in Chinese, also used as a metaphor for somebody who is mischievous and shrewdly calculating.
* the Tiger Stream: a stream not far from East Wood Temple. As is said, tigers could be heard in the hills when one sees off a guest by the stream.

## 窜夜郎于乌江留别宗十六璟

君家全盛日,
台鼎何陆离!
斩鳌翼娲皇,
炼石补天维。
一回日月顾,
三入凤凰池。
失势青门傍,
种瓜复几时?
犹会众宾客,
三千光路歧。
皇恩雪愤懑,
松柏含荣滋。
我非东床人,
令姊忝齐眉。
浪迹未出世,
空名动京师。
适遭云罗解,
翻谪夜郎悲。
拙妻莫邪剑,
及此二龙随。
惭君湍波苦,
千里远从之。
白帝晓猿断,
黄牛过客迟。
遥瞻明月峡,
西去益相思。

## Farewell to Tsung Sixteen at the Crow River When I'm Exiled to Nightboy

Those days your family did flower,
And high above enjoyed great power.
Your sires helped Nüwa, Turtle slayed;
To fix Heaven hued rocks were made.
Much favored by the moon and sun,
Three times state affairs you have run.
Although sometimes power you may lose,
Are you like Shao who melons grows?
Thousands of guests still come to you;
The broad road so packed seems to glow.
When Lord does you exonerate,
All cypresses and pines look great.
I'm not the one in the east bed;
To your sister I have been wed.
Tho I'm drifting like thistledown,
My vain name has spread in the town.
Released from jail not long ago,
Exiled to Nightboy, I now go.
Like Moyeh Sword my wife's with me;
How ashamed I am and shall be!
You o'ercome hardship while you may,
And have seen me a long long way.
In Whitegod monkeys no more cry;
In front of Ox Gorge travelers hie.
Looking at Moon Gorge there afar,
In West here more homesick we are!

* the Crow River: the biggest river in Kuichow, the right branch of the Long River at its upper reaches, once named the Black River.
* Nüwa: the goddess of creation in ancient Chinese mythology. As said, she made seventy things every day, used yellow clay to make humans in imitation of her own image, and created a marital system for humans. When Heaven and earth cracked, she cut off the legs of a giant turtle to support skies and melt colorful stones to mend them, saving humans from the disaster. In this poem, Nüwa is used as a metaphor for Empress Wu (A.D. 624 – A.D. 705), the first female sovereign in Chinese history.
* Shao: referring to P'ing Shao, Lord Eastridge in the Ch'in dynasty, who was degraded as a commoner to grow melons out of town.
* melon: a trailing plant of the gourd family, or its fruit. There are two genera, the muskmelon and the watermelon, each with numerous varieties, growing in both tropical and temperate zones.
* cypresses and pines: two similar kinds of evergreen trees often mentioned together in China, a symbol of rectitude, nobility and longevity in Chinese culture.
* the one in the east bed: referring to Hsichih Wang (A.D. 303 – A.D. 379), a highborn calligrapher in the Eastern Chin dynasty, regarded as the Sage of Handwriting. When Chien Hsi (A.D. 269 – A.D. 339), a minister of the Eastern Chin, sent a hanger-on to the Wang's to select a son-in-law. All the young men in the House dressed up in order to leave a good impression, only Hsichih stayed in his east bed, his belly exposed. Hsichih outshone the others for his care-free attitude.
* Nightboy: once the biggest kingdom founded by southern barbarians in the malarial southwest existing from the Warring States period to the Han dynasty. In 27 B.C., Nightboy was wiped out by Han and was made a county.
* Moyeh: one of two renowned ancient swordsmen, i.e., Kanchiang and Moyeh. They were once collected by Huan Lei in the West Chin dynasty. He gave Kanchiang to his friend Hua Chang and kept Moyeh. But Kanchiang was lost after Chang was murdered. After Lei's death, when his son Lei Hua passed by Yanp'ing Ford, all of a sudden, Moyeh jumped off his waist to the water to join its partner Kanchiang, and the two swords turned into two dragons.
* Whitegod: an ancient city, located near present-day Double Gain (Ch'ungch'ing). It is famous in history as the place where Pei Liu, the Emperor of Shu, died in the Three Kingdoms Period (A.D. 220 – A.D. 280).
* Ox Gorge: below Mt. Ox, 25 kilometers southwest of South Ch'eng County.
* Moon Gorge: a gorge in Pa County, the main urban area of today's Double Gain (Ch'ungch'ing).

## 留别龚处士

龚子栖闲地，
都无人世喧。
柳深陶令宅，
竹暗辟疆园。
我去黄牛峡，
遥愁白帝猿。
赠君卷葹草，
心断竟何言。

## Farewell to Kung, Member of Staff

The place where you live at leisure
No worldlings visit for pleasure.
Like T'ao's mansion with willows deep,
Like P'i's garden where bamboos peep.
To Yellow Ox Gorge I will go;
The monkeys in Whitegod feel blue.
This Siberian cocklebur grass
Is my gift, heartbreaking, alas.

* T'ao: referring to Poolbright T'ao (A.D. 352 – A.D. 427), a verse writer, poet, and litterateur in the Chin dynasty, and the founder of Chinese idyllism, who was once the magistrate of P'engtse.
* P'i's garden: the earliest private garden recorded.
* Yellow Ox Gorge: Ox Gorge, a gorge of the Long River.
* Whitegod: an ancient city built by Shu Lordson (? – A.D. 36) in the Western Han dynasty, located near present-day Double Gain (Ch'ungch'ing). Shu Loedson heard

that there was a well called White Crane in the town, wherefrom white mist in the shape of a dragon often rose to the sky, and he regarded it as a symbol of his ascension to the throne, so he crowned himself as White God or White Emperor.

* cocklebur: a low branching, rank weed (genus *Xanthium*) of the composite family, with hard ovoid or oblong two-celled burs about an inch long.

# 赠别郑判官

窜逐勿复哀,
惭君问寒灰。
浮云本无意,
吹落章华台。
远别泪空尽,
长愁心已摧。
二年吟泽畔,
憔悴几时回。

## Farewell, a Verse to Judge Cheng

My exile cannot be expressed;
Your concern makes me more depressed.
The cloud high above floats alone
And is off Movement Palace blown.
Far away, I feel my tears dried;
Sadness has hollowed my inside.
I've strolled the river for two years;
Homeward my haggard yearning peers.

* Movement Palace: also known as Movement Height (Huachang T'ai), a resort built for King Spirit of Ch'u in 535 B.C., more than 33 meters high and more than 52 meters wide at the base, destroyed in the confusion of war. This colossal building has been commended as the first height in the world, located near Dragon Bay in today's Hupei Province.

## 黄鹤楼送孟浩然之广陵

故人西辞黄鹤楼，
烟花三月下扬州。
孤帆远影碧空尽，
唯见长江天际流。

## Seeing Off Haojan Meng to Broadridge at Yellow Crane Tower

Yellow Crane to my old friend now says bye;
Amid March catkins, to Yangchow he'll go.
The lonely sail fades to merge with the sky;
Lo, beside Heavens the Yangtze does flow.

* Haojan Meng: Haojan Meng (A.D. 689 – A.D. 740), a renowned pastoral poet, Pai Li's good friend, ranking next to Pai Li and Fu Tu in the entire galaxy of the poets of the glorious T'ang Empire, but unfulfilled officially, he lived in reclusion almost all his life.
* Broadridge: an alternative name for Yangchow, a land of Wu in the Spring and Autumn period, belonging to Stripfour (576 B.C.– 484 B.C.), who declined the throne and farmed in Broadridge. It became the most prosperous port city in the T'ang dynasty because of the Peking-Hangchow Canal dug by the previous dynasty and it was a waterland like today's Venice, attracting businessmen, travelers, monks and courtesans from every part of the country and the world.
* Yellow Crane: Yellow Crane Tower, a famous tower built by Wu in A.D. 223, located on the top of Mt. Snake, overlooking the Long River, in present-day Wuhan, Hupei Province.
* catkin: a deciduous scaly spike of flowers, as in the willow, an image of helpless drifting or wandering in Chinese literature.
* Yangchow: alias Broadridge, an important city in today's Chiangsu Province, the greatest port in China and the centre of luxury trades in the T'ang dynasty.

## 将游衡岳过汉阳双松亭留别族弟浮屠谈皓

秦欺赵氏璧,
却入邯郸宫。
本是楚家玉,
还来荆山中。
丹彩泻沧溟,
精辉凌白虹。
青蝇一相点,
流落此时同。
卓绝道门秀,
谈玄乃支公。
延萝结幽居,
剪竹绕芳丛。
凉花拂户牖,
天籁鸣虚空。
忆我初来时,
蒲萄开景风。
今兹大火落,
秋叶黄梧桐。
水色梦沅湘,
长沙去何穷。
寄书访衡峤,
但与南飞鸿。

## Farewell to My Cousins Buddha and T'anhao, Passing Two-Pine Pavilion in Hanshine on the Way to Mt. Scale

Ch'in wanted the jade from Chao's Lord;
In Hantan's palace it was stored.
At first by the State of Ch'u owned,
To Mt. Chaste it was then returned.
Its red colors flow to the blue;
The white rainbow gleams to its glow.
The jade's been by bluebottles stained;
We've been to such a place detained.
In the Word you are so excellent;
With the dark you are so eloquent.
Beneath the trailers I abide;
Around the bamboo blooms grin wide.
The window strokes the petals chill;
The nature hears the vacuum shrill.
I remember when I came first,
The grape blossoms in the wind burst.
Big Fire has vanished, gone away;
Yellow parasol tree leaves sway.
I dreamed of the picturesque land;
How vast, there stretches Long Sand.
Send me letters to Mt. Scale, please;
Trust it to the southbound wild geese.

\* Ch'in: the Ch'in State or the State of Ch'in (905 B.C.- 206 B.C.), one of the most powerful vassal states in the Spring and Autumn period, which developed into the first

unified regime of China, i.e. the Ch'in Empire.
* the jade from Chao's Lord: referring to the jade found on Mt. Chaste by Ho Pien. It originally belonged to the State of Ch'u, and was given as a gift to King of Chao. The State of Ch'in wanted it by cheating, but Hsiangju Lin, a renowned statesman and diplomat of Chao safely sent it back.
* Chao: the State of Chao (403 B.C.- 222 B.C.), a vassal state in the Spring and Autumn period, one of the Seven Powers in the Warring States period.
* Hantan: the capital of Chao.
* Ch'u: a vassal state of Chough, one of the powers in the Warring States period, conquered and annexed by Ch'in in 223 B.C.
* bluebottle: a blowfly (family *Callephoridae*) with a metallic-blue or -green abodomen. The fly, especially the bluebottle, is a nasty slanderer in Chinese culture, like a section of a verse from *The Book of Songs* reads: "Upon the hazels o'erthere, / Alight the buzzing flies. / Those mean men you trust ne'er, / They estrange us with lies."
* the Word: referring to Tao if transliterated, the most significant and profoundest concept in Chinese philosophy. The Word is identifiable with the Word or Logos in the West in terms of either Christianity or the philosophy of Heraclitus, as there is an enormous amount of common ground in the cosmologies and doctrines concerning the most fundamental matters such as "the Word is the One" and "God is the One", and the personalization of Being, the progenitor of finite spirits, which are subordinate kinds of Being or merely appearances of the Divine, the One.
* bamboo: a tall, tree-like or shrubby grass in tropical and semi-tropical regions, a symbol of integrity and altitude, one of the four most important images in Chinese literature, which are wintersweet, orchid, bamboo and chrysanthemum. Plankbridge Cheng (1693 - 1765), A Ching poet, speaks of its character in a poem Bamboo Rooted in the Rock: "You bite the green hill and ne'er rest. / Roots in the broken crag, you grow, / And stand erect although hard pressed. / East, west, south, north, let the wind blow."
* grape: any grapevine yielding grapes, smooth-skinned, edible, juicy, berrylike fruit, introduced to China by Chien Chang (164 B.C.- 114 B.C.) in the Han dynasty.
* Big Fire: a star, what is Antares in Western astronomy.
* Mt. Scale: one of the Five Mountains in China, located in Hunan Province, along with Mt. Ever in Shanhsi, Mt. Arch in Shantung, Mt. Flora in Sha'anhsi, and Mt. Tower in Honan.
* wild goose: an undomesticated goose that is caring and responsible, taken as a symbol of benevolence, righteousness, good manner, wisdom and faith in Chinese culture.

# 留别贾舍人至二首

## Farewell to Secretary Chia, Two Poems

### 其 一

大梁白云起，
飘摇来南洲。
徘徊苍梧野，
十见罗浮秋。
鳌抃山海倾，
四溟扬洪流。
意欲托孤凤，
从之摩天游。
凤苦道路难，
翱翔还昆丘。
不肯衔我去，
哀鸣惭不周。
远客谢主人，
明珠难暗投。
拂拭倚天剑，
西登岳阳楼。
长啸万里风，
扫清胸中忧。
谁念刘越石，
化为绕指柔。

### No. 1

White clouds over Great Beam float and

Are blown to the shoal in South Land.
They linger, and o'er the fields green
Ten times La Phu's autumn have seen.
Whales and turtles turn waves upside
Down and all the sea surges with tide.
On the phoenix I would rely,
And with her I would cruise the sky.
The phoenix knows the hard way, alack;
To Queenknoll she does now fly back.
She would not away from me fly;
"Sorry, sorry", it does there cry.
I'd go away and thank host mine;
Pearls should not be cast before swine.
Stroking my sword called On Sky Rest,
I climb up Mountshine Tower from west.
For thousands of miles the wind blows
And from my chest sweeps off my woes.
The hard Yüehstone, one never deems,
Can be soft like cotton, it seems.

* Great Beam: the capital of Way, not far from present-day K'aifeng, Honan Province.
* La Phu: an attractive mountain in Kuangtung where Surge Ko (Hung Ko), a hermit in the Chin dynasty, used to live in seclusion.
* whale: a cetaceous mammal of fish-like form, especially one of the larger pelagic species, as distinguished from dolphins and porpoises.
* Pearls should not be cast before swine: It is from an idiom. Cast pearls before a swine, which means "do not give precious things to someone who doesn't know the value of them". A pearl is a lustrous, calcareous concretion deposited in the shell of a mollusk, largely used as a gem or regarded as treasure while a swine is an omnivorous mammal having a long mobile snout and cloven hoofs, which, concerned only with eating and sleeping to a Chinese eye, has no sense for beauty or value.
* stroking my sword: alluding to Pai Li's swordsmanship. In his early youth, Pai Li exhibited a swashbuckling penchant, took to knight-errantry, and learned

swordmanship from Min P'ei, the universally acknowledged swordsman in the T'ang dynasty, and as Pai Li boasted, he even cut down several combatants with his cutlass.
* Mountshine Tower: an ancient tower located in today's Yüehshine, Hunan Province.
* Yüehstone: Yüehstone Liu (A.D. 276 - A.D. 318), an official of the West Chin, loyal to the royal house, regarded as hard stone.
* cotton: the soft, white seed hairs filling the seedpods of various shrubby plants of the mallow family, originally native to the tropics, introduced to China in the Western Han dynasty.

## 其 二

秋风吹胡霜，
凋此檐下芳。
折芳怨岁晚，
离别凄以伤。
谬攀青琐贤，
延我于北堂。
君为长沙客，
我独之夜郎。
劝此一杯酒，
岂惟道路长。
割珠两分赠，
寸心贵不忘。
何必儿女仁，
相看泪成行。

## No. 2

The fall wind blows northern frost here;
Under the eaves the blossoms sear.
I pluck a spray, it's late, I'm old;
As we now part, it's chill, I'm cold.
I'm among the saints by mistake;
And sit in North Hall without sake.
A guest, you will in Long Sand stay;
To Nightboy I will go away.
Do have a toast, finish this cup,
Not for the long trip, down and up.
I will cut the pearl into two,

Either to stand for our heart true.
Don't do like children kind but weak,
Whose sad tears from their sockets leak.

* Long Sand: a vassal state of Han, present-day Ch'angsha, Hunan Province.
* Nightboy: once the biggest kingdom founded by southern barbarians in the southwest existing from the Warring States period to the Han dynasty. When a Han envoy visited Nigthboy, the king asked: "Which is bigger, Nigthboy or Han?" This self-important question has been a laughing stock ever since. In 27 B.C., Nightboy was wiped out by Han and was made a county.
* pearl: a smooth, lustrous, usually white and bluish-gray, calcareous concretion deposited in layers around a central nucleus in the shells of various mollusks or oysters, and largely used as a gem, medicine or given as a gift, a metaphor for the dearest one, a representation of nobility, purity and dignity in Chinese culture.

# 渡荆门送别

渡远荆门外，
来从楚国游。
山随平野尽，
江入大荒流。
月下飞天镜，
云生结海楼。
仍怜故乡水，
万里送行舟。

# Farewell at Mt. Chastegate

I'll go afar from Mt. Chastegate
For a travel in the Ch'u State.
The mountains end at the vast plain;
The river flows to the wild main.
The moon shines, a mirror to be;
The clouds build a high tower at sea.
O my dear mountain and water
See my boat go far and farther.

* Mt. Chastegate: Chingmen if transliterated, an area of military significance in the middle of present-day Hupei Province.
* the Ch'u State: a vassal state of Chough, one of the powers in the Warring States period, conquered and annexed by Ch'in in 223 B.C.

## 闻李太尉大举秦兵百万出征东南懦夫请缨冀申一割之用半道病还留别金陵崔侍御十九韵

秦出天下兵，
蹴踏燕赵倾。
黄河饮马竭，
赤羽连天明。
太尉杖旄钺，
云旗绕彭城。
三军受号令，
千里肃雷霆。
函谷绝飞鸟，
武关拥连营。
意在斩巨鳌，
何论鲙长鲸。
恨无左车略，
多愧鲁连生。
拂剑照严霜，
雕戈鬘胡缨。
愿雪会稽耻，
将期报恩荣。
半道谢病还，
无因东南征。
亚夫未见顾，
剧孟阻先行。
天夺壮士心，
长吁别吴京。
金陵遇太守，

倒屣相逢迎。
群公咸祖饯,
四座罗朝英。
初发临沧观,
醉栖征房亭。
旧国见秋月,
长江流寒声。
帝车信回转,
河汉复纵横。
孤凤向西海,
飞鸿辞北溟。
因之出寥廓,
挥手谢公卿。

## Marshal Li Commands a Million Royal Troops to March Southeast and I Request for an Assignment to Do My Bit. Ill, I Write This Farewell Verse to Royal Servant Ts'ui, Prefect of Gold Hill

The royal troops with all might run;
The trodden Yan and Chao are won.
War steeds have the River drunk dry;
Red plumes of arrows light the sky.
The marshal his scepter waves high;
Flags flap around P'eng, far and nigh.
The troops get the marshal's order,
And stand there, threatening thunder.
Over Case Dale no more birds fly;
The barracks Wu's Pass occupy.

The giant turtles they tend to slay,
Not caring those herrings astray.
I don't have Leftcart's tactics rare,
Or else Chunglien Lu's writing flair.
My sword stroked does to the frost shine;
The warriors hold halberds in line.
I'll revenge the Summit disgrace,
And try best to repay His grace.
I return half way as diseased,
Not able to fight in the east.
Not having Yafu's good regard,
I can't go though I can fight hard.
God will divest me of my will;
With a long sigh, I'll leave Gold Hill.
Here Prefect Ts'ui I bump into;
He greets me, right foot in left shoe.
All gents toast to me farewell wine;
At all tables are talents fine.
I start from Blue Fane and its monk,
And in Beat Foe Bower lie so drunk.
The old state sees the chill moon glow;
The Yangtze with coldness does flow.
Lo, the Big Dipper turns around
And sees the Milky Way profound.
The phoenix to West Sea does cry;
The wild goose to North Brine does fly.
I would go above the broad sky
While waving to you all good bye.

* Yan and Chao: two northern vassal states or northern area in general.
* the River: the Yellow River, the second longest river in China.

* P'eng: an alternative name for Hsuchow, the second largest city in today's Chiangsu Province.
* Case Dale: an ancient pass located to the east of the capital, and Lint'ao to the west.
* Chunglien Lu: Chunglien Lu (cir. A.D. 305 - A.D. 245), a political strategist, a sophist. He once helped Lord Plain of Chao successfully persuade the State of Way to fight together against Ch'in. After that, he declined the awards given by Lord Plain and went away.
* the Summit disgrace: In the Spring and Autumn period, King of Yüeh surrendered at Mt. Summit. The later generations refer it as disgrace of a perished state.
* Yafu: referring to Yafu Chou (199 B.C.- 143 B.C.), a general of great reputation in the Han dynasty, who once felt relieved when hearing that Chümeng did not fight against him.
* Gold Hill: referring to Nanking, one of the most well-known ancient capitals in China, once the capital of Wu, Chin, and many other states or kingdoms, which flourished immensely with increasing trade and travel.
* Blue Fane: a Wordist temple in Gold Hill where the ancients bid farewell.
* Beat Foe Bower: an ancient kiosk in Gold Hill built by Hsieh Shih, a general in the Eastern Chin dynasty.
* the Yangtze: the Yangtze River, the lower reaches of the Long River.
* the Big Dipper: the Dipper, a constellation composed of seven bright stars, which looks like a spoon in the sky.
* the Milky Way: a luminous band circling the heavens composed of stars and nebulae; the Galaxy.

## 别韦少府

西出苍龙门，
南登白鹿原。
欲寻商山皓，
犹恋汉皇恩。
水国远行迈，
仙经深讨论。
洗心向溪月，
清耳敬亭猿。
筑室在人境，
闭门无世喧。
多君枉高驾，
赠我以微言。
交乃意气合，
道因风雅存。
别离有相思，
瑶瑟与金樽。

## Farewell to Sheriff Wei

West, I go through Blue Dragongate;
South, I climb the Plain of Whitedeer
I would look for the Elders Great,
His Majesty's grace I revere.
To the water land I'll depart,
Where books of the Word I'll devour.
To the stream moon I wash my heart,

Hearing apes crying at the bower.
I build my hut in the world here;
It's so quiet once I close the door.
You've come many times to show care,
And present me with words and more.
Trustworthiness can win one's heart,
Hence the mould elegantly fine.
Love grows intense as we're apart;
I quench my thirst with verse and wine.

* Blue Dragongate: the gate of royal palace of Han.
* the Word: the Creator, the primordial and perpetual force in and beyond the universe. The Word is identifiable with the Word or Logos in the West, as there is an enormous amount of common ground in the two cosmologies and the doctrines concerning the most fundamental matters such as "the Word is the One" and "God is the One", and the personalization of Being, the progenitor of finite spirits, which are subordinate kinds of Being or merely appearances of the Divine, the One.
* Plain of Whitedeer: located to the southeast of Long Peace.
* the Elders Great: referring to the Four Gray Heads of the Han dynasty, Emperor Highsire's think tank.

## 南陵别儿童入京

白酒新熟山中归，
黄鸡啄黍秋正肥。
呼童烹鸡酌白酒，
儿女嬉笑牵人衣。
高歌取醉欲自慰，
起舞落日争光辉。
游说万乘苦不早，
著鞭跨马涉远道。
会稽愚妇轻买臣，
余亦辞家西入秦。
仰天大笑出门去，
我辈岂是蓬蒿人。

## Leaving Southridge for the Capital, Goodbye to My Children

I return from the hills, spirit newly brewed;
The yellow chicks look fat, pecking at food.
Cooked chicken and spirit my kids bring in;
They pull me by the clothes and widely grin.
Singing aloud, drunk, I myself enhance;
To vie with the setting sun glow, I dance.
Your Majesty, it's quite late in the day,
Please gallop your horse along the broad way.
A vain wife from Summit on Chu looked down;
Saying: I'll go to Ch'in, leaving my town.

> I go outdoor, laughing toward the sky;
> I'm not a wren in the bush, how can I?

* Summit: referring to Mt. Summit, the K'uaichi Mountains in present-day Chechiang Province, where Worm convened a summit attended by vassal lords, hence the name.
* Chu: referring to Maich'en Chu, a senior official in the Han dynasty, who once lived by selling firewood. When he was a woodcutter, his wife left him because of their poverty. By diligent study, however, he became prefect of K'uaichi; and his wife, who had sunk to destitution, begged to be allowed to rejoin him. But he replied, "If you can pick up spilt water, you may return", whereupon his wife went and hanged herself.
* Ch'in: the Ch'in State or the State of Ch'in (905 B.C.- 206 B.C.), enfeoffed as a dependency of Chough by King Piety of Chough in 905 B.C and enfeoffed as a vassal state by King Peace of Chough in 770 B.C. In the ten years from 230 B.C. to 221 B.C., Ch'in wiped out the other six powers and became the first unified regime of China, i.e. the Ch'in Empire.
* wren: any of numerous small passerine birds, having short rounded wings and a short tail, symbolizing something unimportant.

## 别　山　僧

何处名僧到水西，
乘舟弄月宿泾溪。
平明别我上山去，
手携金策踏云梯。
腾身转觉三天近，
举足回看万岭低。
谑浪肯居支遁下，
风流还与远公齐。
此度别离何日见，
相思一夜暝猿啼。

## Farewell to a Hill Monk

From where are you coming west of the rill?
In the Ching Stream your moonlit oar you ply.
At dawn you take leave of me for the hill;
With a Zen stick you climb the path cloud high.
You turn around and feel the sky is near;
You lift your foot and down all hills you peer.
In banter Chih Tun can't with you compare;
Your great talent can match Farsight's great flair.
When can we meet again as now I leave;
A sleepless night, I may hear monkeys grieve.

\* the Ching Stream: a stream in Hsuan, an old historic city in today's Anhui Province.
\* Zen: a kind of performance of quietude in a form of meditation or contemplation.

When Sanskrit jana was spread to China, it was translated as Zan or Zen for this kind of practice. In the T'ang dynasty, educated Chinese were imbued with Zen, and many of them were associated with Zen monks and spent much time in Zen monasteries.

* Chih Tun: Chih Tun (A.D. 314 – A.D. 366), a high monk, Buddhist and litterateur in the Eastern Chin dynasty.

## 赠别王山人归布山

王子析道论，
微言破秋毫。
还归布山隐，
兴入天云高。
尔去安可迟？
瑶草恐衰歇。
我心亦怀归，
屡梦松上月。
傲然遂独往，
长啸开岩扉。
林壑久已芜，
石道生蔷薇。
愿言弄笙鹤，
岁晚来相依。

## Farewell to Wang the Hermit When I Go Back to Mt. Cloth

My friend, on the Word you expound;
Though little is said, it's profound.
You'll retire to the mountains soon;
Your spirit soar up to the moon.
A few more days can you here stay
Lest the ganoderma decay?
My heart also seeks hermits' ease;
I oft dream of moonlit pine trees.

> With pride you go there all alone;
> To build a room you chop up stone.
> Bleak has become the woody vale;
> Roses grow rank on the stone trail.
> With you I'd the flute and cranes play;
> In winter we'll together stay.

* Mt. Cloth: probably referring to the old county that was instituted in 214 B.C. in today's Kuanghsi Province.
* the Word: referring to Tao if transliterated, the most significant and profoundest concept in Chinese philosophy. According to Laocius's *The Word and the World*: "The Word is void, but its use is infinite. O deep! It seems to be the root of all things."
* ganoderma: Ganoderma Lucidum Karst in Latin, a grass with an umbrella top, a pore fungus, used as medicine and tonic in China.
* rose: any of a genus of shrubs of the rose family, characteristically with prickly stems, alternate compound leaves, and five-parted, usually fragrant flowers or red, pink, white, yellow, etc., having many stamens. It is often used as a metaphor for beauty or love.
* crane: one of a family of large, long-necked, long-legged, heronlike birds allied to the rails, a symbol of integrity and longevity in Chinese culture, only second to the phoenix in cultural importance.

## 江夏别宋之悌

楚水清若空，
遥将碧海通。
人分千里外，
兴在一杯中。
谷鸟吟晴日，
江猿啸晚风。
平生不下泪，
于此泣无穷。

## Farewell to Chiht'i Sung from Riversummer

Ch'u's water as clear as can be
Links up with the faraway sea.
I'll be thousands of miles from you;
My interest's just in the brew.
On fine days cuckoos sweetly trill;
To late wind river monkeys shrill.
Never before have I shed tear;
Without stop, sadly I cry here.

* Riversummer: an ancient town tracing back to 350 B.C. when Sha-e was established and was officially renamed Riversummer in A.D. 589, one of the three towns that constitutes Wuhan, now called Chianghsia District under Wuhan.
* Ch'u: a vassal state of Chough, one of the most powerful states in the Warring States period, conquered and annexed by Ch'in in 223 B.C.
* cuckoo: the bird of homesickness in Chinese culture. It is said that during the Shang

dynasty, Cuckoo (Yü Tu), a caring king of Shu, abdicated the throne due to a flood and lived in reclusion. After his death, he, the human Cuckoo, turned into a bird cuckoo, wailing day and night, shedding tears and blood.

# 古近体诗二十一首
## Old-new Rhythmic Poetry, 21 Poems

# 南 阳 送 客

斗酒勿为薄，
寸心贵不忘。
坐惜故人去，
偏令游子伤。
离颜怨芳草，
春思结垂杨。
挥手再三别，
临歧空断肠。

# Farewell to Southshine

Wine's ne'er too little, drink it dry;
Don't forget the thing that we start.
Now you're going away I sigh;
So heavy is my vagrant's heart.
Of the senseless grass I complain,
And splash my rues to the willow.
I wave my hand once and again,
Immersed in my parting sorrow.

---

* Southshine: an alternative name for South Town, in today's Honan Province.
* willow: any of a large genus of shrubs and trees related to the poplars, having generally narrow leaves, smooth branches, and often long, slender, pliant, and sometimes pendent branchlets, a symbol of farewell or nostalgia in Chinese culture. The best image is in *Vetch We Pick*, a verse in *The Book of Songs*, which reads like this: When we left long ago, / The willows waved adieu. / Now back to our home town, / We meet snow falling down.

# 送张舍人之江东

张翰江东去，
正值秋风时。
天清一雁远，
海阔孤帆迟。
白日行欲暮，
沧波杳难期。
吴洲如见月，
千里幸相思。

## Seeing Off Secretary Chang to the East

Like that Han Chang east you now go
Just when the autumn wind does blow.
A wild goose flies far, the sky vast;
The broad sea dwarfs the lonely mast.
Now setting west is the white sun;
When can we meet while the waves run?
Over Wu's Shoal shines the same moon,
To which our love song we can croon.

* Han Chang: a litterateur in the Western Chin dynasty. He, a native from Kusu (today's Soochow), resigned from his office in Loshine because he missed perch and water shield in his hometown.
* wild goose: an undomesticated goose that is caring and responsible, taken as a symbol of benevolence, righteousness, good manner, wisdom and faith in Chinese culture.
* Wu's Shoal: an allusion to Yannien Yan's line. From Wu's Shoal I begin to oar.

# 送王屋山人魏万还王屋(并序)

　　王屋山人魏万,云自嵩宋沿吴相访,数千里不遇。乘兴游台越,经永嘉,观谢公石门。后于广陵相见,美其爱文好古,浪迹方外,因述其行而赠是诗。

仙人东方生,
浩荡弄云海。
沛然乘天游,
独往失所在。
魏侯继大名,
本家聊摄城。
卷舒入元化,
迹与古贤并。
十三弄文史,
挥笔如振绮。
辩折田巴生,
心齐鲁连子。
西涉清洛源,
颇惊人世喧。
采秀卧王屋,
因窥洞天门。
揭来游嵩峰,
羽客何双双。
朝携月光子,
暮宿玉女窗。
鬼谷上窈窕,
龙潭下奔潈。
东浮汴河水,
访我三千里。

逸兴满吴云,
飘飖浙江汜。
挥手杭越间,
樟亭望潮还。
涛卷海门石,
云横天际山。
白马走素车,
雷奔骇心颜。
遥闻会稽美,
一弄耶溪水。
万壑与千岩,
峥嵘镜湖里。
秀色不可名,
清辉满江城。
人游月边去,
舟在空中行。
此中久延伫,
入剡寻王许。
笑读曹娥碑,
沉吟黄绢语。
天台连四明,
日入向国清。
五峰转月色,
百里行松声。
灵溪咨沿越,
华顶殊超忽。
石梁横青天,
侧足履半月。
眷然思永嘉,
不惮海路赊。
挂席历海峤,

回瞻赤城霞。
赤城渐微没，
孤屿前峣兀。
水续万古流，
亭空千霜月。
缙云川谷难，
石门最可观。
瀑布挂北斗，
莫穷此水端。
喷壁洒素雪，
空濛生昼寒。
却思恶溪去，
宁惧恶溪恶。
咆哮七十滩，
水石相喷薄。
路创李北海，
岩开谢康乐。
松风和猿声，
搜索连洞壑。
径出梅花桥，
双溪纳归潮。
落帆金华岸，
赤松若可招。
沈约八咏楼，
城西孤岩峣。
岩峣四荒外，
旷望群川会。
云卷天地开，
波连浙西大。
乱流新安口，
北指严光濑。

钓台碧云中,
邈与苍岭对。
稍稍来吴都,
裴回上姑苏。
烟绵横九疑,
漭荡见五湖。
目极心更远,
悲歌但长吁。
回桡楚江滨,
挥策扬子津。
身著日本裘,
昂藏出风尘。
五月造我语,
知非儓儗人。
相逢乐无限,
水石日在眼。
徒干五诸侯,
不致百金产。
吾友扬子云,
弦歌播清芬。
虽为江宁宰,
好与山公群。
乘兴但一行,
且知我爱君。
君来几何时?
仙台应有期。
东窗绿玉树,
定长三五枝。
至今天坛人,
当笑尔归迟。
我苦惜远别,

茫然使心悲。
黄河若不断，
白首长相思。

# Seeing Off Wan Way, Hermit of Mt. Kinghouse Back to Kinghouse (With a Foreword)

Wan Way, Hermit of Mt. Kinghouse, says that he has gone thousands of miles from Sung via Wu, but fails to see me. He goes on to tour T'ai, Yüeh, and Good E'er and pays a visit to Hsieh's Stonegate and finally sees me in Broadridge. He loves literature and antiquity and lives as a hermit. I hereby give an account of his tour, hence this poem.

The hermit Newmoon East by name
Surfs all clouds and seas as his game.
Riding a dragon, he has gone,
Just his spirit lingering on.
You are named after Lord of Way,
And there in Liao and She you stay.
Your spirit has come from the One;
Your virtue's saintly, so well done.
I began writing at thirteen;
My poems did brilliantly sheen.
My eloquence did Pa subdue;
And in smartness I could beat Lu.
You went to Loshine in the west,
Surprising the world of unrest.
On Mt. Kinghouse you drew pure air;
Into Heaven's Gate you did stare.

An immortal, you toured sometime
And the clouded peaks you did climb.
At dawn you rose with Moonglow;
At dusk you watched her window.
The deep Ghost Vale you did explore,
Watching Black Abyss rise and pour.
From east you crossed the Pien to me
Having come for three thousand li.
Your elegance like a cloud flown
Was to the Ch'ient'ang River blown.
Between Hang and Yüeh you did wave
And at Camphor Bower saw tides rave.
The breaks washed up the stone on high,
Like clouds rushing all o'er the sky.
Like white horses drawing a cart,
Like rash thunders crashing a heart.
As told, Mt. Summit's like a dream;
You played ripples of the Yeh Stream.
All the ranges and all the dales
Showed in the lake and there left trails.
Through all lyric scenes you rowed;
The river town with vigor glowed.
You strolled to approach the moon fair
While your boat cruised the moving air.
Against the vast landscape you soared
And Wang's and Hsu's relics explored.
You read Fair Ts'ao' epitaph verse
By Ts'ai for great piety of hers.
You toured Mt. Heaven, Mt. Four Bright,
State Clean Fane, and every good sight.
On Five Peaks you watched the moon shine

And heard a sough from pine to pine.
You went across Yüeh's Spirit Stream
And leaped over the Towering Beam.
The stone bridge seemed to link the sky;
Your foot trod half the moon awry.
Then Good E'er appeared in your mind;
You cared not the sea route did wind.
Isle after isle you sailed ahead
And then saw Red Town beaming red.
While Red Town vanished without trace,
An isle appeared there, face to face.
The water flew along as e'er;
The bower vacant faced the moon fair.
Mt. Red Silk Clouds looked high and great;
Spectacular was Mt. Stone Gate.
Waterfalls hung from the Dipper;
Where was the source of the water?
Water splashed down the sky like snow,
Giving off a cold misty glow.
If you would go to the Vile Stream,
You feared not how vile it might seem.
Across seventy shoals it roared;
Water and stone each to each poured.
Where was North Sea who paved a route?
And where was Hsieh who a verse wrote?
The pine zephyrs and monkeys' wails
Filled all the caves, trenches and dales.
Wintersweet Flower Bridge you passed thru;
The two streams into one sea flew.
When at Gold Coast dropping your sail,
You felt Red Pine give you a hail.

Shen crooned on Eight-Chants Tower so high
That rose against the town's west sky.
The west sky saw from everywhere
Rivers flow into this place here.
Clouds rolled on between sky and land;
Waves rushed and did westward expand.
You went thru Newmouth with the flow
And came to Torrent of Tight Glow.
The mound from where Tight Glow fished then
Stood against the green hill and glen.
You came to Capital of Wu
And with leisure climbed Mt. Kusu.
Mt. Nine Doubts was wrapped in haze;
The five lakes surged with swirls and sways.
You thought deep gazing with wide eyes
And sang sadly between long sighs.
With cheer, you went upstream on board
And moored at River Yangtze Ford.
Japanese kimono you wore;
Your demeanor struck one with awe.
Fifth moon, you had a talk with me;
You were not a fool, not a pea.
Our encounter's been a great one,
Like gurgles over pebbles run.
Though we got on with vassal lords,
We did not do that for gold hoards.
My brilliant friend Man Yang by name
For his rule had won a good fame.
Tho he's River Calm's magistrate,
He's the same as a hermit great.
If you will, to him we can go

To show to him our friendship true.
How long have you travelled around?
You should go back to Fairy Mound.
The green tree by your window sways
With three or five newly grown sprays.
The one atop Mt. Kinghouse there
Should be laughing: You're late as e'er.
If to ask you to stay I try,
I may make you helplessly sigh.
I will miss you with my gray hair,
Like the River that flows for e'er.

* Wan Way: an adorer of Pai Li.
* Mt. Kinghouse: a house-like mountain in Shanhsi Province, one of the Ten Mountains of Wordist Attractions.
* Sung: an ancient town in present-day Honan Province.
* Wu: referring to the area south of the Yangtze River.
* T'ai: referring to present-day Linhai, Chechiang.
* Yüeh: referring to present-day Shaohsing, Chechiang.
* Good E'er: referring to present-day Wenchow, Chechiang.
* Hsieh: referring to Lingyün Hsieh (A.D. 385 – A.D. 433), a highborn poet, Buddhist and traveler, famous for landscape poems.
* Stonegate: a famous mountain in Good E'er. When Lingyün Hsieh governed Good E'er, he once visited the mountain and composed poems there.
* Broadridge: an alternative name for Yangchow, an important city in today's Chiangsu Province, the greatest canal port in China and the centre of luxury trades in the T'ang dynasty.
* Newmoon East: referring to Shuo Tungfang (154 B.C.– 93 B.C.), a jocular and witted official serving Lord Martial of Han. According to legend, he knew magic and rode a dragon.
* Lord of Way: referring to Piwan, a minister of the State of Chin in the Spring and Autumn period, who was entitled Lord of Way for he helped the king of Chin wipe out three states.
* Liao: referring to present-day Liaoch'eng, Shantung Province.

* She: referring to present-day Tsaip'ing, Shantung Province.
* dragon: a fabulous serpent-like giant winged animal, a symbol of benevolence and sovereignty in Chinese culture.
* the One: a Wordist term indicating natural changes or the unification of everything. Similarly, in the West, God is the One, Self-subsisting Reality. The One in the West and the One in the East are actually one, identifiable though in different languages.
* Pa: referring to Pa T'ien, a debater of Ch'i in the Warring States period. He was good at debating but defeated by Chunglien Lu.
* Lu: referring to Chunglien Lu (305 B.C.- 245 B.C.), a sophist of Ch'i in the late Spring and Autumn period.
* Loshine: Loyang if transliterated, the eastern capital and the second largest city in the T'ang dynasty, with a population of about 0.8 million.
* Heaven's Gate: indicating mountains that immortals dwell.
* Moonglow: a fair boy in legend.
* Ghost Vale: a vale in present-day Honan Province where Lord Ghost Vale, the founder of the school of Ghost Vale, used to live. The school was rather mysterious, whose students were erudite enough to have a wide coverage of knowledge including diplomacy, geography and the Word of Nature.
* Black Abyss: a deep valley in present-day Tengfeng, Honan Province.
* Pien: referring to the Pien River in present-day Honan Province.
* li: a unit of measurement of length. One li is equal to 500 meters.
* the Ch'ient'ang River: originally the Zigzag River (Chechiang lierally in Chinese), originating from Mt. Holdjade (Huaiyü) that is 1,600 meters above sea level in Anhui Province and floweing to East Sea at Hangchow Bay, the biggest river in Chechiang Province.
* Hang and Yüeh: referring to Hangchow and Shaohsing.
* Camphor Bower: an ancient courier post in Hangchow.
* Mt. Summit: referring to the K'uaichi Mountains in present-day Chechiang Province, where Worm convened a summit attended by vassal lords, hence the name.
* the Yeh Stream: or Joyeh Stream, a stream in the south of present-day Shaohsing, flowing into Lake Mirror. It's said that West Maid did her laundry here.
* Wang and Hsu: referring to Hsichih Wang (A.D. 303 – A.D. 379), a highborn calligrapher in the Eastern Chin dynasty, regarded as the Sage of Handwriting, and Mai Hsu, a highborn litterateur. They used to live at the Shan Stream.
* Fair Ts'ao: Fair Ts'ao (A.D. 130 – A.D. 143), a girl from Summit in the Eastern Han dynasty, who died for salvaging her drowned father, well remembered for her filial piety.

* Ts'ai: referring to Yung Ts'ai (A.D. 133 – A.D. 192), who wrote Fair Ts'ao's epitaph, a renowned official, litterateur, and calligrapher in the Eastern Han dynasty.
* Mt. Heaven: a mountain in today's Chechiang Province.
* Mt. Four Bright: an offset of Mt. Heaven Terrace.
* State Clean Fane: a Buddhist temple on Mt. Heaven.
* Five Peaks: peaks of Mt. Heaven in present-day Chechiang Province.
* Yüeh's Spirit Stream: located at Mt. Heaven.
* the Towering Beam: the highest peak of Mt. Heaven.
* Red Town: Mt. Red Town, a mountain in today's Chechiang Province.
* Mt. Red Silk Clouds: a mountain in present-day Chinyün, Chechiang.
* Mt. Stone Gate: a mountain in present-day Ch'ingt'ien, Chechiang.
* the Vile Stream: a stream in present-day Chechiang Province, which is famous for magnificence.
* North Sea: referring to Yung Li (A.D. 678 – A.D. 747), an official, poet and calligrapher in the T'ang dynasty, once prefect of North Sea. He built a lane when he was a magistrate of Chechiang.
* Wintersweet Flower Bridge: unidentified. One speculation is that it is in present-day Chinhua, Chechiang Province.
* Gold Coast: a mountain said to be where Red Pine became immortal, located in present-day Chinhua, Chechiang.
* Red Pine: According to legend, Red Pine is an immortal.
* Shen: Yüeh Shen, a poet in the State of Ch'i in the Southern dynasty.
* Eight-Chants Tower: a tower in today's Chinhua, Chechiang Province. After Shen wrote Eight-Changs Poems there, the tower was renamed Eight-Chants Tower.
* Newmouth: an affluent of the Ch'ient'ang River.
* Torrent of Tight Glow: where Tight Glow, as known as Tsuling Yan (39 B.C.– A.D. 41), a renowned hermit in the Han dynasty, used to fish.
* Kusu: an alternative name for Soochow.
* Mt. Nine Doubts: the mountain where Hibiscus was buried. It was so named because it confused people by similar peaks and landscape.
* the five lakes: referring to T'ai Lake in present day Chiangsu.
* River Yangtze Ford: an ancient Yangtze River crossing, in present-day Eecheng, Chiangsu Provence.
* Man Yang: Man Yang (53 B.C.– A.D. 18), Hsiung Yang if transliterated, born in Silkton, present-day Chengt'u, Ssuch'uan, a great scholar, rhymed prose writer and official in the Han dynasty, whose *The Great One* had a deep influence on works of later generations. According to *History of the Han Dynasty*, when other officials

flattered those in power, only Man Yang kept to himself to write his philosophical work, *The Great One*.

* Rivers Calm: referring to present-day Nanking, Chiangsu Province.
* the River: the Yellow River, the second longest river in China, the birthplace of Chinese civilization.

## 送当涂赵少府赴长芦

我来扬都市，
送客回轻舠。
因夸楚太子，
便观广陵涛。
仙尉赵家玉，
英风凌四豪。
维舟至长芦，
目送烟云高。
摇扇对酒楼，
持袂把蟹螯。
前途倘相思，
登岳一长谣。

## Seeing Off Chao, Sheriff of Tangt'u, to Long Reed

Why do I come here to the town?
To see you back with currents down.
As Prince of Ch'u saw tides of yore,
We've come to listen to waves roar.
You're a great one, from Chao's good seed,
And higher than Four Gallants you fly.
You row all the way to Long Reed,
To see clouds off to the blue sky.
Waving your fan to a wine tower,
You take hold of crab pincers long.

> Whene'er you miss me, at that hour,
> Do climb uphill and sing a song.

* Four Gallants: referring to the four outstanding childes in the Warring States period, known as Lord Mengch'ang of Ch'i, Lord Plain of Chao, Lord Faithridge of Way and Lord Chunshen of Ch'u.
* Long Reed: Ch'anglu if transliterated, located in present-day Nanking.
* crab: any of various decapods with four pairs of legs, one pair of pincers, a flattish shell, a short, broad abdomen folded under its thorax.

## 送友人寻越中山水

闻道稽山去,
偏宜谢客才。
千岩泉洒落,
万壑树萦回。
东海横秦望,
西陵绕越台。
湖清霜镜晓,
涛白雪山来。
八月枚乘笔,
三吴张翰杯。
此中多逸兴,
早晚向天台。

## Seeing Off My Friend to Mid-Yüeh

You'll head for Mt. Summit I hear,
Which well suits Hsieh, your kind, your peer.
Springs falling down from rocks you'll see
And valleys are filled, tree by tree.
East Sea looks at Emperor Mound;
Westridge does Yüeh Platform surround.
Lake Mirror gleams with frost, so bright;
The breakers rush like mountains white.
The eighth moon there awaits verse thine;
While like Han you enjoy best wine.
So many things may interest you;

Mt. Heaven is where you must go.

* Mid-Yüeh: referring to present-day Shaohsing, Chechiang Province.
* Mt. Summit: referring to the K'uaichi Mountains in present-day Chechiang Province, where Worm convened a summit attended by vassal lords, hence the name.
* Hsieh: referring to Lingyün Hsieh (A.D. 385 - A.D. 433), a highborn poet, official, Buddhist, idyllist and traveler, famous for landscape poems.
* Emperor Mound: Emperor Mound (2377 B.C.- 2259 B.C.), Yao if transliterated. Divine and noble, Mound has been regarded as one of Five Lords in ancient China.
* Lake Mirror: 1) a clear river, also recorded in other literature, but unidentified now; 2) a large reservoir built in the Han dynasty, higher than the fields and the fields higher than the sea, 310 li in circumference.
* Yüeh Platform: a mound where Kouchien (520 B.C.- 465 B.C.), King of Yüeh, used to look into far distance.
* Han: referring to Han Chang, a litterateur in the Western Chin dynasty.
* Mt. Heaven: a mountain in Chechiang Province.

## 送族弟凝之滁求婚崔氏

与尔情不浅，
忘筌已得鱼。
玉台挂宝镜，
持此意何如。
坦腹东床下，
由来志气疏。
遥知向前路，
掷果定盈车。

## Seeing Off a Cousin of Mine to Make a Proposal to Miss Ts'ui

We are good and good friends, aren't we?
Once you are blessed, you forget me!
With gems and mirrors, your bride's price,
How do you feel, so nice, so nice?
A brilliant bridegroom like your kind
Will be in roses drunk you'll find.
A man like you, handsome and smart,
Will have fruit thrown to fill your cart.

---

\* rose: any of a genus of shrubs of the rose family, characteristically with prickly stems, alternate compound leaves, and five-parted, usually fragrant flowers or red, pink, white, yellow, etc., having many stamens. It is often used as a metaphor for beauty or love.

# 送友人游梅湖

送君游梅湖，
应见梅花发。
有使寄我来，
无令红芳歇。
暂行新林浦，
定醉金陵月。
莫惜一雁书，
音尘坐胡越。

# Seeing Off My Friend to Lake Wintersweet

You'll tour Lake Wintersweet and play
With blossoms bursting on each spray.
Send me a few, send some to me
In case red blooms fade from the tree.
To Riverside Wood I'll go soon,
And uphill, I'll toast to the moon.
Send a letter oft to me, pray
Lest we'd be kept so far away.

* Lake Wintersweet: a lake near Gold Hill, the capital of many dynasties in Chinese history.
* Riverside Wood: Five kilometers from Gold Hill, today's Nanking, the capital of Chiangsu Province.

# 送崔十二游天竺寺

还闻天竺寺，
梦想怀东越。
每年海树霜，
桂子落秋月。
送君游此地，
已属流芳歇。
待我来岁行，
相随浮溟渤。

## Seeing Off Ts'ui Twelve to Visit Temple of Bamboo Divine

With Temple of Bamboo Divine,
East Yüeh appears oft in dreams mine.
Each year trees seaside with frost on,
From Luna laurel seeds fall down.
Now to that place you go and play,
The blooms should have dried to decay.
Next year I'll be there to join you
To chase the tide and see the view.

* Temple of Bamboo Divine: built in A.D. 597 in the Sui dynasty, an important temple in Hangchow.
* East Yüeh: the area in present-day Chechiang Province.
* laurel: laurus nobilis, an evergreen shrub with aromatic, lance-shaped leaves, yellowish flowers, and succulent, cherry-like fruit, a symbol of glory usually in the form of a crown or wreath of laurel to indicate honor or high merit, especially when

one had passed Grand Test in ancient China. In Chinese mythology, there is a laurel tree on the moon, and it would never fall even though Kang Wu, a banished immortal, has kept cutting it.

## 送杨山人归天台

客有思天台,
东行路超忽。
涛落浙江秋,
沙明浦阳月。
今游方厌楚,
昨梦先归越。
且尽秉烛欢,
无辞凌晨发。
我家小阮贤,
剖竹赤城边。
诗人多见重,
官烛未曾然。
兴引登山屐,
情催泛海船。
石桥如可度,
携手弄云烟。

## Seeing Off Yang, a Hermit, to Mt. Heaven

Mt. Heaven often haunts your mind;
The way rolls east and does east wind.
The autumn river hears tides roar;
The moon does chill the brightened shore.
You've played in Ch'u, tired, for some time;
Your dream may have come to South Clime.

In candlelight now we just play,
Tomorrow no good bye we'd say.
I have a nephew working there,
A magistrate, Red Town's good mayor.
A scholar like you he respects;
A clean one, nothing he neglects.
You may climb hills with him when free
Or when with impulse cruise the sea.
Upon Stone Bridge if you dare stand,
You two may chase clouds hand in hand.

* Mt. Heaven: a mountain in Chechiang Province.
* Ch'u: the State of Ch'u, a vassal state of Chough, one of the seven powers in the Warring States period, conquered and annexed by Ch'in in 223 B.C.
* Red Town: a town three kilometers from Mt. Heaven County.

## 送温处士归黄山白鹅峰旧居

黄山四千仞，
三十二莲峰。
丹崖夹石柱，
菡萏金芙蓉。
伊昔升绝顶，
下窥天目松。
仙人炼玉处，
羽化留馀踪。
亦闻温伯雪，
独往今相逢。
采秀辞五岳，
攀岩历万重。
归休白鹅岭，
渴饮丹砂井。
凤吹我时来，
云车尔当整。
去去陵阳东，
行行芳桂丛。
回溪十六度，
碧嶂尽晴空。
他日还相访，
乘桥蹑彩虹。

## Seeing Off Wen, a Hermit, to His Old Residence at White Goose Peak of Mt. Yellow

Mt. Yellow so high scrapes the blue,
Where stand lotus peaks thirty two.
Red crags stone columns do enfold,
Like lotus buds, like lilies gold.
I once climbed to the top, so high,
O'erlooking pines on Mt. Sky-eye.
Immortals made elixirs here;
As spirits, they left traces mere.
I hear there's a Wordist called Wen;
You may go there and meet him then.
For magic herbs, he left Five Hills,
And has tried all crags, caves and rills.
When tired, on Mt. White Goose he'll dwell;
And thirsty, drink from Red Sand Well.
I will come when phoenixes call;
In Cloud Cart we'll tour Heaven's Hall.
East of Mt. Ridgeshine we may go,
Where laurel blooms with fragrance blow.
The creek flows on with bends sixteen;
The sky is clear and the peaks green.
I will come back some other day
To Bow Bridge neath a rainbow ray.

* Mt. White Goose: a landmark of Mt. Yellow.
* Mt. Yellow: located in Anhui Province, one of the most famous mountains in China

with natural, literary, and cultural attractions, featured with wondrous pines, clouds and hotsprings. As is said, Lord Yellow used to make elixirs here.
* Mt. Sky-eye: a mountain near Hangchow with two lakes atop like two eyes, hence the name.
* Wordist: one who believes in or professes belief of Wordism, the doctrines declared by Laocius (571 B.C.- 471 B.C.). In the T'ang dynasty, while Confucianism remained the guiding principle of state and social morality, Wordism had gathered an incrustation of mythology and superstition and became popular with both the court and the commoners. Laocius, the founder, was claimed by the reigning dynasty as its remote progenitor and was honored with an imperial title, Emperor Dark One.
* Wen: referring to Po Wen, a Wordist in the Spring and Autumn period.
* Five Hills: referring to the Five Mountains.
* Red Sand Well: a hot spring at the east foot of Mt. Yellow.
* Phoenix: In Chinese myths, phoenixes, auspicious birds, unlike ordinary ones, only perch on parasol trees, and only eat bamboo shoots and pearly stone.
* Cloud Cart: a vehicle for immortals to ride.
* Mt. Ridgeshine: a mountain in Anhui where Sir Glare became immortal. Sir Glare, fond of fishing, once caught a white dragon. He felt scared and released it. Later, Glare got a white fish with a prescription in its body. He found all the ingredients and took them as elixir. Three years later, the white dragon came to pick him up onto a hill.
* Bow Bridge: the most dangerous spot of Mt. Yellow, with two crag rocks going against each other to form a natural bridge.

# 送方士赵叟之东平

长桑晓洞视，
五藏无全牛。
赵叟得秘诀，
还从方士游。
西过获麟台，
为我吊孔丘。
念别复怀古，
潸然空泪流。

# Seeing Off Chao to East Peace

You introspect and see all through,
Five vitals seen, so clear and true.
Tho such a knack you can command,
With Wordists you still tour the land.
When you come to Unicorn Height,
Pay homage to Confucius' Site.
While we depart, the past I miss;
So helplessly, my tears flow like this.

* East Peace: a prefecture in the T'ang dynasty, today's East Peace County, Shantung Province.
* Wordist: one who believes in or professes belief of Wordism, the naturalist doctrines declared by Laocius (571 B.C.- 471 B.C.).
* Unicorn Height: or Unicorn Mound, a tower built in the Han dynasty to memorize those who made great contributions to the empire.
* Confucius: Confucius (551 B.C.- 479 B.C.), a renowned thinker, educator and

statesman in the Spring and Autumn period, born in the State of Lu, who was the founder of Confucianism. Through his righteousness, optimism and enterprising spirit, he has greatly influenced the character of the Chinese people from generation to generation. He is one of the few leaders who based their philosophy on the virtues that are required for the day-to-day living. His philosophy centered on personal and governmental morality, correctness of social relationships, justice and sincerity.

## 送韩准裴政孔巢父还山

猎客张兔置,
不能挂龙虎。
所以青云人,
高歌在岩户。
韩生信英彦,
裴子含清真。
孔侯复秀出,
俱与云霞亲。
峻节凌远松,
同衾卧盘石。
斧冰嗽寒泉,
三子同二屐。
时时或乘兴,
往往云无心。
出山揖牧伯,
长啸轻衣簪。
昨宵梦里还,
云弄竹溪月。
今晨鲁东门,
帐饮与君别。
雪崖滑去马,
萝径迷归人。
相思若烟草,
历乱无冬春。

## Seeing Off Ch'un Han, Cheng P'ei, and Ch'aofu Kung Back to the Hills

The hunter that a hare trap spread
Could not round tigers up instead.
Those who would go to a blue cloud
Should live in hills and sing aloud.
So great, Han, how brilliant you are!
So cool, P'ei, now you aim afar!
So bright, Kung, you stand out and high!
You are all near clouds in the sky!
The old pine tree you overbear;
On the stone the same quilt you share!
Ice axed, you drink as water flows;
You three have but two pairs of shoes.
Now and then you would write a rhyme
And feel so free from time to time.
From officials you keep away,
And sing aloud there, come what may.
I came back to hills in my dream,
With clouds and bamboo in the stream.
This morn at the gate in the east,
I made camp so I could you feast.
Beware of snow, the horse may fail;
And dense vines sprawl all o'er the trail.
O missing does a trouble bring,
That bothers one winter or spring.

\* Ch'un Han: unidentified.

* Cheng P'ei: unidentified.
* hare: a rodent (genus *Lepus*) with cleft upper lip, long ears, and long hind legs, characterized by its timidity and swiftness, habitating woodland, farmland or grassland.
* tiger: a large carnivorous feline mammal of Asia, with vertical black wavy stripes on a tawny body and black bars or rings on the limbs and tail, praised as king of all animals.
* Kung: referring to Ch'aofu mentioned in the title, an official in the T'ang dynasty, who once lived in seclusion with the poet.

## 送杨少府赴选

大国置衡镜，
准平天地心。
群贤无邪人，
朗鉴穷情深。
吾君咏南风，
衮冕弹鸣琴。
时泰多美士，
京国会缨簪。
山苗落涧底，
幽松出高岑。
夫子有盛才，
主司得球琳。
流水非郑曲，
前行遇知音。
衣工剪绮绣，
一误伤千金。
何惜刀尺馀，
不裁寒女衾。
我非弹冠者，
感别但开襟。
空谷无白驹，
贤人岂悲吟。
大道安弃物，
时来或招寻。
尔见山吏部，
当应无陆沉。

## Seeing Off Yang, a County Sheriff, to His Appointment

Our country's like a mirror bright
That does reflect all people right.
No courtier plays an evil part;
The fairness wins everyone's heart.
His Majesty *The South Wind* sings
And for great virtue plucks the strings.
Good times make people good and sweet,
In Capital great ones I meet.
Weak grass grows there beside a creek;
Tall pines stand high atop a peak.
Now you are talented, so bright,
Your boss has you like a gem right.
Unlike Cheng's tunes clean water flows;
You'll meet one that your value knows.
When cutting silk, you should beware;
A mistake costs much gold as e'er.
Do save some while scissors you hold
To sew a piece for girls who're cold.
I'm not one who plays a vile part;
Now parting I speak out my heart.
No white ponies there in void vales;
No sage is given to sad wails.
The great Word does nothing disdain;
If blessed, I may be used again.
A personnel head when you see,
You will for sure sing praise of me.

* *The South Wind*: an ancient song whose composer is said to be Hibiscus.
* Cheng's tunes: tunes from the State of Cheng (806 B.C.- 375 B.C.), a vassal state that was famous for its economy, legal system, democracy and culture of poetry and music.
* pony: a small horse of any of a number of breeds, usually not over 58 inches, high at the withers.
* the Great Word: the Word, Tao if transliterated, the most significant and profoundest concept in Chinese philosophy. According to Laocius's *The Word and the World*: "The Word is void, but its use is infinite. O deep! It seems to be the root of all things."

## 对雪奉饯任城六父秩满归京

龙虎谢鞭策,
鸾鸾不司晨。
君看海上鹤,
何似笼中鹑。
独用天地心,
浮云乃吾身。
虽将簪组狎,
若与烟霞亲。
季父有英风,
白眉超常伦。
一官即梦寐,
脱屣归西秦。
窦公敞华筵,
墨客尽来臻。
燕歌落胡雁,
郢曲回阳春。
征马百度嘶,
游车动行尘。
踌躇未忍去,
恋此四座人。
饯离驻高驾,
惜别空殷勤。
何时竹林下,
更与步兵邻。

## Farewell to Uncle Six, Who Has Finished His Tenure at Jen and Is Going Back to the Capital

A tiger needs no spur to go;
A phoenix does not for dawn crow.
The crane that over the sea flies
Is not like a caged quail that cries.
My heart's between Heaven and earth;
The floating cloud bespeaks my worth.
An officer although you are,
From vanity fair you're afar.
Now Uncle Six, you're great, so great,
Exceeding White Brows, the first rate.
Rank or wealth just like a dream goes;
You go back west, doffing your shoes.
Tou has prepared a feast for you;
All writers come to say adieu.
The feast song attracts Huns' wild geese;
*Spring Snow* rings to a warm spring breeze.
Your horse has neighed and neighed to start,
Kicking up dust, drawing your cart.
You hesitate and stay as such,
Because you love your friends so much.
It's your horse and cart that would stay,
Have one more cup, one more cup, pray.
When you come back to Bamboo Wood,
Live as good neighbors here we should.

- * phoenix: an auspicious bird of great beauty, unique of its kind, which was supposed to live five or six hundred years before consuming itself by fire, rising again from its ashes to live through another cycle, a symbol of immortality. In Chinese mythology, the phoenix only perches on phoenix trees, i.e. firmiana, only eats firmiana fruit, and only drinks sweet spring water, and this mythic bird appears only in times of peace and sagacious rule.
- * crane: one of a family of large, long-necked, long-legged, heronlike birds allied to the rails, a symbol of integrity and longevity in Chinese culture, only second to the phoenix in cultural importance.
- * White Brows: referring to Liang Ma (A.D. 187 – A.D. 222), an official of Shu in the Three Kingdoms period, who was the eldest and the most virtuous of his five brothers.
- * wild goose: an undomesticated goose that is caring and responsible, taken as a symbol of benevolence, righteousness, good manner, wisdom and faith in Chinese culture.
- * *Spring Snow*: a Han Conservatoire tune.
- * Bamboo Wood: a bamboo grove where Chi Juan used to play.

## 鲁郡尧祠送吴五之琅琊

尧没三千岁，
青松古庙存。
送行奠桂酒，
拜舞清心魂。
日色促归人，
连歌倒芳樽。
马嘶俱醉起，
分手更何言。

## Seeing Off Wu Five to Ivory at Mound's Shrine in Lu

Three thousand years ago Mound died;
The pines stay by the temple's side.
We bid farewell with laurel wine;
The dance does purify heart mine.
Elapse of time calls: Hurry up;
Let me sing and fill one more cup.
Me drunk, the horse begins to neigh;
Now parting, I've no more to say.

* Ivory: Ivory Mound, Langya T'ai if transliterated, a coastal mound built by Emperor First in present-day Shantung Province.
* Mound: Mound (2377 B.C.- 2259 B.C.), Yao if transliterated. Divine and noble, Mound has been regarded as one of Five Lords in ancient China.
* laurel: laurus nobilis, an evergreen shrub with aromatic, lance-shaped leaves, yellowish flowers, and succulent, cherry-like fruit, a symbol of glory usually in the

form of a crown or wreath of laurel to indicate honor or high merit, especially when one had passed Grand Test, i.e. Civil Service Examinations for selecting government officials, in ancient China. In Chinese mythology, there is a colossal laurel tree that is more than 1,500 meters tall on the moon, and it would never fall even though Kang Wu, a banished immortal, has kept cutting it.

## 鲁郡尧祠送窦明府薄华还西京

朝策犁眉骃,
举鞭力不堪。
强扶愁疾向何处,
角巾微服尧祠南。
长杨扫地不见日,
石门喷作金沙潭。
笑夸故人指绝境,
山光水色青于蓝。
庙中往往来击鼓,
尧本无心尔何苦。
门前长跪双石人,
有女如花日歌舞。
银鞍绣毂往复回,
簸林蹶石鸣风雷。
远烟空翠时明灭,
白鸥历乱长飞雪。
红泥亭子赤阑干,
碧流环转青锦湍。
深沉百丈洞海底,
那知不有蛟龙蟠。
君不见绿珠潭水流东海,
绿珠红粉沉光彩。
绿珠楼下花满园,
今日曾无一枝在。
昨夜秋声阊阖来,
洞庭木落骚人哀。
遂将三五少年辈,

登高远望形神开。
生前一笑轻九鼎，
魏武何悲铜雀台。
我歌白云倚窗牖，
尔闻其声但挥手。
长风吹月度海来，
遥劝仙人一杯酒。
酒中乐酣宵向分，
举觞酹尧尧可闻。
何不令皋繇拥篲横八极，
直上青天挥浮云。
高阳小饮真琐琐，
山公酩酊何如我。
竹林七子去道赊，
兰亭雄笔安足夸。
尧祠笑杀五湖水，
至今憔悴空荷花。
尔向西秦我东越，
暂向瀛洲访金阙。
蓝田太白若可期，
为余扫洒石上月。

# Seeing Off Pohua Tou, a Magistrate, West to Capital at Mound's Shrine in Lu

At dawn I spur my yellow horse;
To wave the whip, I have no force.
Where shall I go, so ill, suffering all pain?
I come to visit Mound's Shrine in clothes plain.
The willow twigs sweep up the shade aground;

The stone gate gushes for a pool profound.
My friend has found the best for me I smile;
The green of hills the blue sky does beguile.
The people come and go to pray for bliss;
Mound has no mind for that, why do like this?
Before the gate two stone men for long kneel;
The singers and dancers to all appeal.
So many carts and chariots quake the ground,
Like thunders' rumbling, forest shaking sound.
The distant smoke and waves now dim, now glow;
White seagulls flutter like fluttering snow.
Scarlet pavilion, ruby balustrade,
Azure whirligig, emerald cascade.
What's there at the bottom of the ocean?
Some dragons there stirring up a motion?
Don't you espy the emerald abyss flows to the sea;
Green pearls, red powder have all ceased to be.
The blue tower saw the court have blossoms on,
Today there's no spray left, all colors gone.
Last night from west blew a chill autumn sough;
Lake Cavehall surged and leaves fell, sad enow.
With several young friends of the same kind,
I climb high, gaze afar, so free of mind.
When living, if Ts'ao could have won the throne,
Would his wives to Bronze Sparrow Platform croon?
White Cloud I sing, leaning on the window;
Hearing me, you wave to me to echo.
When a wind blows the moon here from the brine,
We should toast to the saints a cup of wine.
In the depth of the night so drunk we feel,
And toast to Mound but does he know our zeal?

If so, he'd order Potter to take up a broom and try
To sweep off the floating clouds from the sky.
The Highshine Pool feast was nothing, so small;
Could Hillman, drunk, compare with me at all?
The Seven at Bamboo Wood were less blessed;
The Orchid Kiosk writings are not the best!
The pool at Mound's Shrine outshines Five Lakes blue,
But lotus blooms there have withered to skew.
I'm going to East Yüeh and you West Ch'in,
And I'll search Isle for hermits out and in.
If in Blue Field and Venus we meet soon,
Please clean the stone for me to shoo the moon.

* Mound's Shrine: 2.5 kilometers from today's Linfen, Shanhsi Province.
* seagull: a kind of sea bird, any gull or large tern, a symbol of clean integrity. The seagulls in the Wordist book *Sir Line* (Liehtzu) are particularly sensitive to impurity of motive and will make friends only with the completely guileless and disinterested.
* dragon: Though variously understood as a large reptile, a marine monster, a jackal and so on in Western culture, it has been esteemed as a fabulous serpent-like giant winged animal, a totem of the Chinese nation and a symbol of benevolence and sovereignty in Chinese culture.
* Lake Cavehall: a large lake in today's Hunan Province.
* Bronze Sparrow Platform: a mound built by Ts'ao Ts'ao in the Three Kingdoms period.
* Potter: or Moor Potter (cir. 2219 B.C.- 2113 B.C.), Kaoyao if transliterated, a law enforcer of Mound, an important statesman, thinker, educator and lawyer in prehistoric China, one of the Four Saints in Old China, the other three being Mound, Hibiscus, and Worm.
* Hillman: referring to the fifth son of T'ao Shan, one of the Seven Sages of the Bamboo Grove in the Chin dynasty. He was as gentle and graceful as his father. When he was an official, the nation was falling apart and other officials were worried and depressed. Hillman, however, lived a casual life. Every time he hung out, he would hold a banquet and get drunk at the Highshine Pool.
* the Seven at Bamboo Wood: referring to the Seven Sages of Bamboo Groves.
* Orchid Kiosk: a kiosk where Wang Hsichih, the most famous calligrapher, held a

poem party.
* the Five Lakes: referring to Lake T'ai and the other four lakes around. As legend goes that, Li Fan (536 B.C.- 448 B.C.), a renowned statesman, strategist, economist and Wordist in the Spring and Autumn period, changed his name to live in seclusion among the Five Lakes after he helped the State of Yüeh wipe out Wu.
* Blue Field: Mt. Blue Field, a mountain 15 kilometers away from Blue Field County under today's Hsi-an, Sha'anhsi Province, famous for jade mined there, called Blue Field Jade.
* Venus: Mt. Venus, a mountain in present-day Sha'anhsi, the main peak of Ch'in Ridge, the highest peak east of Blue Sea-Tibetan Plateau in China.

## 金乡送韦八之西京

客自长安来，
还归长安去。
狂风吹我心，
西挂咸阳树。
此情不可道，
此别何时遇。
望望不见君，
连山起烟雾。

## Seeing Off Wei Eight to Capital from Goldton

From Capital you did depart
And back to Capital you'll be.
The mad wind blows west to my heart
And hangs it on Allshine tree.
My feelings I cannot subdue;
When can we gather I'm agog.
Gazing hard, I fail to see you;
O'er the mountains rises a fog.

* Capital: Long Peace or Ch'ang'an if transliterated, the capital of the T'ang Empire, with one million inhabitants, the largest walled city ever built by man, and a cosmopolis swarming with dignitaries from all over the world and the center of world religions, Buddhism, Confucianism, Wordism, Nestorianism, Zoroastrianism, and even Islamism represented by Saracens. It is now Hsi-an, West Peace literally, the capital of Sha'anhsi Province with a population of about ten million.

## 送薛九被谗去鲁

宋人不辨玉，
鲁贱东家丘。
我笑薛夫子，
胡为两地游？
黄金消众口，
白璧竟难投。
梧桐生蒺藜，
绿竹乏佳实。
凤凰宿谁家，
遂与群鸡匹。
田家养老马，
穷士归其门。
蛾眉笑躃者，
宾客去平原。
却斩美人首，
三千还骏奔。
毛公一挺剑，
楚赵两相存。
孟尝习狡兔，
三窟赖冯谖。
信陵夺兵符，
为用侯生言。
春申一何愚，
刎首为李园。
贤哉四公子，
抚掌黄泉里。
借问笑何人，

笑人不好士。
尔去且勿喧，
桃李竟何言。
沙丘无漂母，
谁肯饭王孙？

# Seeing Off Slandered Hsüeh Nine to Lu

Sung folks don't jewels recognize;
Lu men e'en Confucius despise.
How simple, now I laugh at you,
Why'd you lobby there to and fro?
Many mouths melt gold into none;
Who knows white jade, who is the one?
With phoenix trees caltrop does grow;
No fruit is seen on green bamboo.
Phoenixes, where can they abide?
With ducks and hens or by their side.
Of an old nag T'ien once took care;
Poor scholars all would with him fare.
His belle a cripple did disdain;
So all hangers-on left Prince Plain.
And then the prince cut off her head;
Back to him his three thousand sped.
To show his sharp sword there was Mao,
So two states survived, Ch'u and Chao.
Mengch'ang did well treat all his men,
So Feng proposed many a den.
Prince Faithridge grasped the warring seal,
As Hou heartened him a great deal.

How foolish, what a foolish man!
Shen was cruelly murdered by Yüan.
The four men, princes debonair,
Do laugh in the netherworld there.
May I ask who they laugh at then?
They laugh at incredulous men!
Now all of you, you may go out;
Good fruit nothing worries about.
No Washing Mother is o'er there;
Where could he have a humble fare?

* Sung: the State of Sung (cir. 1039 B.C.- 286 B.C.), a vassal state of Chough, a dukedom, its capital being Shang Knoll (Shangch'iu).
* Confucius: Confucius (551 B.C.- 479 B.C.), a renowned thinker, educator and statesman in the Spring and Autumn period, born in the State of Lu, who was the founder of Confucianism and who had exerted profound influence on Chinese culture.
* caltrop: any of various plants (especially *Tribulus terrestris*) with spiny heads or fruit that entangle the feet.
* duck: a web-footed, broad-billed water bird of the *Anatinae* family comprising fresh water and wood ducks, the sea and bay ducks, and the mergansers, a symbol of success in passing Grand Test, i.e., the imperial civil examination in ancient China.
* T'ien: referring to Tsufang T'ien, a Wordist from the State of Way. He bought an old nag for he pitied it.
* Prince Plain: Chao Sheng, a prince of Chao and a renowned statesman in the Warring States period. A belle of the prince once laughed at a cripple, but the prince did not punish her. Knowing that, the hangers-on all left him.
* Mao: referring to Sui Mao (285 B.C.- 228 B.C.), a lobbyist from Chao who recommended himself to visit Ch'u and gained his fame by making an alliance between Ch'u and Chao.
* Mengch'ang: a lord of Ch'i and one of the Four Childes in the Warring States period.
* Feng: referring to Feng Yüan, a hanger-on of Mengch'ang. He asked a lot from his lord but did a lot for him in return.
* Prince Faithridge: a prince of Way, one of the Four Childes in the Warring States period.
* Hou: referring to Ying Hou (? -257 B.C.), a hermit who lived as a porter of Smooth

Gate of the State of Way and became a hanger-on of Prince Faithridge. When threatened by the troops of Ch'in, Chao asked Faithridge for help. Hou suggested stealing the military tally so that Way's army was under Faithridge's command. In this way, Faithridge successfully saved Hantan.

* Shen: referring to Lord Shen or Lord Chunshen, that is, Hsieh Huang (314 B.C.-238 B.C.), a renowned statesman and one of the Four Childes in the Warring States period.
* Yüan: Yüan Li (? - 228 B.C.), a minister of Ch'u. He first married his sister to Lord Shen and then to king of Ch'u when she was pregnant. After King of Ch'u passed away, he murdered Shen and took over the power.
* Washing Mother: referring to the laundry lady who provided Hsin Han with food when the latter was poor.

## 单父东楼秋夜送族弟沈之秦
### （时凝弟在席）

尔从咸阳来，
问我何劳苦。
沐猴而冠不足言，
身骑土牛滞东鲁。
沈弟欲行凝弟留，
孤飞一雁秦云秋。
坐来黄叶落四五，
北斗已挂西城楼。
丝桐感人弦亦绝，
满堂送君皆惜别。
卷帘见月清兴来，
疑是山阴夜中雪。
明日斗酒别，
惆怅清路尘。
遥望长安日，
不见长安人。
长安宫阙九天上，
此地曾经为近臣。
一朝复一朝，
发白心不改。
屈平憔悴滞江潭，
亭伯流离放辽海。
折翮翻飞随转蓬，
闻弦坠虚下霜空。
圣朝久弃青云士，
他日谁怜张长公。

# Seeing Off Shen, My Cousin, from Shanfu to Capital on an Autumn Night
# (Another Cousin, Ning, Is at the Feast)

You come from Allshine in the west
To ask me with what I'm distressed.
Not like those monkeys' irritable way,
Riding a dusty ox in Lu I'll stay.
Ning will stay here while Shen will go,
Like to Ch'in wild geese flying thru.
I have sat for long and there fall leaves dry;
Over Tower West, the Dipper hangs so high.
The sad string melody saddens each heart;
No friends there in the hall would like to part.
Clear moonlight enters the window to glow.
A mirage like the mount covered with snow.
Tomorrow you'll go, now let's cheer;
The road is full of dust, I fear.
Out at Capital I long stare;
I could see no one over there.
The palace and tower there reach the Ninth Sky;
I used to serve His Majesty nearby.
I did serve there day after day,
So faithful that my hair grew gray.
Like Yüan Ch'ü who the river did deplore;
Like Yin Ts'ui who was exiled east to Liao.
I'm like a bird flying with broken wings,
Which falls down from the frost sky at sad strings.
Since the court has left pure scholars alone,

I'll be like Chang, perhaps, for life unknown.

* Shanfu: a county in present-day Shantung.
* Allshine: the ancient capital of Ch'in, present-day Allshine (Hsienyang), Sha'anhsi Province.
* those monkeys' irritable way: originally implying Yü Hsiang, who showed no patience like monkey wearing a hat.
* Ch'in: the Ch'in State or the State of Ch'in (905 B.C.- 206 B.C.), one of the most powerful vassal states in the Chough dynasty, which developed into the first unified regime of China, i.e. the Ch'in Empire.
* the Dipper: a constellation composed of seven bright stars, which looks like a spoon in the sky.
* Riding a dusty ox: implying the plight of promotion.
* the Ninth Sky: the high sky, the highest of the nine layers of the sky according to Chinese legend.
* Yüan Ch'ü: Yüan Ch'ü (340 B.C.- 278 B.C.), a great patriotic poet and official of Ch'u, the archetype of the incorruptible and faithful minister, repeatedly wronged by the king. His suicide at last by drowning in the Milo River is still commemorated every year throughout China by the Dragon Boat Festival.
* Yin Ts'ui: Yin Ts'ui (? - A.D. 92), an official in the Eastern Han dynasty, exiled after failing in admonishing his superior.
* Chang: referring to Chih Chang, who was too upright to blend with those crafty in the court.

# 送族弟凝至晏堌单父三十里

雪满原野白，
戎装出盘游。
挥鞭布猎骑，
四顾登高丘。
兔起马足间，
苍鹰下平畴。
喧呼相驰逐，
取乐销人忧。
舍此戒禽荒，
微声列齐讴。
鸣鸡发晏堌，
别雁惊涞沟。
西行有东音，
寄与长河流。

# Accompanying My Cousin to Yanku, 15 Miles from Shanfu

The wilderness covered with snow,
My cousin equipped does out go.
A hunter he spurs now to chase;
A mountain he climbs so to gaze.
A hare bumps to the hoof amain;
An eagle whoops down to the plain.
The shouting and running about
Drives one's cares and worries all out.

We'll soon stop, no longer obsessed;
We will sing quietly and then rest.
In Yanku roosters crow: dawn light;
O'er the Lai wild geese cry with fright.
Your journey west rings with my song,
While the river flows all along.

* Yanku: the relics of Yanku can be found north of Yanku Mound Village in today's Hotze, Shantung Province.
* hare: a rodent (genus *Lepus*) with cleft upper lip, long ears, and long hind legs, characterized by its timidity and swiftness, habitating woodland, farmland or grassland.
* eagle: a diurnal bird of prey of the family Accipitridae of worldwide distribution, notable for keen sight and strong flight, usually praised as a hero in Chinese culture.
* rooster: the male of the chicken that struts with pride and crows at dawn. The rooster is often a theme of literature, as is shown in *A Rooster in the Painting* by Pohu T'ang (1470 - 1524), a Ming painter, "Untailored, naturally made its red crown, / The pure snow tiptoes, donning a white gown. / It dare not call, now timid as before; But at its crow all households ope their door."
* the Lai: the Lai River, out of East Gate of Shan County, in today's Shantung Province.
* wild goose: an undomesticated goose that is caring and responsible, taken as a symbol of benevolence, righteousness, good manner, wisdom, and faith in Chinese culture.

## 鲁城北郭曲腰桑下送张子还嵩阳

送别枯桑下，
凋叶落半空。
我行愦道远，
尔独知天风。
谁念张仲蔚，
还依蒿与蓬。
何时一杯酒，
更与李膺同。

## Seeing Off Chang to Towershine at a Crooked Mulberry North of Luton

At the mulberry I bid him bye,
A leaf falls as if from the sky.
My way rolls so far off to bend;
You, so blessed, can the sky ascend.
But you, so cleanly, like Chungwei,
Will in thistle and wormwood stay.
When can we meet and drink a cup,
Like with Ying Li who'd help me up?

* Towershine: name of a temple north of Luton, i.e. today's Chockfull (Ch'üfu), Shantung Province.
* mulberry: the edible, berry-like fruit of a tree (genus *Morus*) whose leaves are valued for silkworm culture, and the tree itself, first cultivated in the drainage area of the Yellow River in China about five thousand years ago.
* Chungwei: Chungwei Chang, a hermit in the Chin dynasty.

* thistle: any of various plants of the composite family, with prickly leaves and heads of white, purple, pink, or yellow flowers.
* wormwood: any of a genus of strong-smelling plants of the composite family, with white or yellow flowers.
* Ying Li: Ying Li (A.D. 110 - A.D. 169), a renowned scholar and official in the Eastern Han dynasty, once being a prefect and a catcher inspector (with an independent 1,200 troops), renowned for his rectitude and justice, worshipped by official-literati all over China.

# 古近体诗四十四首
## Old-new Rhythmic Poetry, 44 Poems

## 送鲁郡刘长史迁弘农长史

鲁国一杯水,
难容横海鳞。
仲尼且不敬,
况乃寻常人。
白玉换斗粟,
黄金买尺薪。
闭门木叶下,
始觉秋非春。
闻君向西迁,
地即鼎湖邻。
宝镜匣苍藓,
丹经埋素尘。
轩后上天时,
攀龙遗小臣。
及此留惠爱,
庶几风化淳。
鲁缟如白烟,
五缣不成束。
临行赠贫交,
一尺重山岳。
相国齐晏子,
赠行不及言。
托阴当树李,
忘忧当树萱。
他日见张禄,
绨袍怀旧恩。

# Seeing Off Liu, a Secretary in Lu to Be a Secretary in Great Farming

A wine cup in the State of Lu
Can't hold a whale surfing the blue.
Athwart Confucius they e'en run,
Let alone a poor common one.
A disc of jade? For little rice!
A bar of gold? A thin plank's price!
Indoors I feel leaves falling down;
Autumn is unlike spring, I frown.
I hear to the west you will plod
To a place neighboring Lake Pod.
A treasured mirror, a pill book
Were buried in a dusty nook.
When Lord Yellow climbed up the sky,
The courtiers with him dropped from high.
Lord Yellow's grace can still be seen,
Because good people there have been.
Lu's silk looks like white clouds, alack,
Though five rolls do not make a pack.
As you start, you give it to me,
A mountain seems a roll to be.
Ch'i's prime minister Yan by name
Gave Tseng words, and I'll do the same.
For a shade one needs a plum tree,
And day lilies make one care-free.
If I can make success one day,
Your great kindness I will repay.

* Great Farming: a county that was established in Han and revoked in the year A.D. 997, in today's Lingpao, Honan Province.
* the State of Lu: the state enfeoffed to Prince of Chough, inherited by his son Firstling Bird, exterminated by Ch'u in 256 B.C.
* Confucius: Confucius (551 B.C.- 479 B.C.), a renowned thinker, educator and statesman in the Spring and Autumn period, born in the State of Lu, who was the founder of Confucianism and who had exerted profound influence on Chinese culture.
* Lake Pod: Lake Tripod. Lord Yellow became immortal at Lake Tripod and rode a dragon to fly to the sky.
* Lord Yellow: alias Cartshaft, the first of the five heavenly gods in myth and the earliest ancestor of Chinese people. It was said that Lord Yellow made a tripod in the Chaste Hills. As the tripod was done, a dragon came down to visit him. He and his 70 or more officials and consorts all rode on the dragon and flew to the sky. In myth, when Lord Yellow and his retinue rode the dragon away, they left some junior officials on earth, who could but pull the dragon's beard in vain. All they got was only a strand of beard and the sword dropped from Lord Yellow.
* Yan: Ying Yan (578 B.C.- 500 B.C.), a minister of Ch'i in the Spring and Autumn period, a statesman, diplomat and ideologist.
* Tseng: referring to Shen Tseng (505 B.C.- 435 B.C.), a renowned ideologist in the Spring and Autumn period, a student of Confucius's and one of the representatives of Confucianism.
* plum: a kind of plant or the edible purple drupaceous fruit of the plant which is any one of various trees of the genus *Prunus*, cultivated in temperate zones.
* day lily: any of several lilyworts, with alnceolate leaves, and large flowers on a round thick scape, usually lasting one day. Two species *H. fulva*, tawny red, and *H. flava*, bright yellow, are commonly cultivated.

## 送族弟单父主簿凝摄宋城主簿至郭南月桥却回栖霞山留饮赠之

吾家青萍剑，
操割有馀闲。
往来纠二邑，
此去何时还。
鞍马月桥南，
光辉歧路间。
贤豪相追饯，
却到栖霞山。
群花散芳园，
斗酒开离颜。
乐酣相顾起，
征马无由攀。

## Seeing Off Ning, My Cousin, Secretary of Shanfu, to Be Secretary of Sung, Stopping South of Moon Bridge and Returning to Mt. Clouds for a Farewell Party

Blue Lotus Sword our gallant plays
So deftly, to thrust, cut or hack.
The two towns see his busy days;
Now leaving, when will he come back?
South of Moon Bridge our steeds we tie;
The crossroads are moonlit to shine.
The worthies will bid you good bye

And come to Mt. Clouds to drink wine.
Though blossoms wither there to dry;
We toast and cheer from heart to heart.
Now feeling drunk, in spirits high,
Who'll get on his horse to depart?

* Shanfu: a county in present-day Shantung.
* Blue Lotus Sword: a precious long sword, more than one meter long, with blue lotus flowers carved on it.
* Mt. Clouds: a mountain two kilometers from Shan County, i.e. Shanfu in present-day Shantung.

# 鲁郡东石门送杜二甫

醉别复几日，
登临遍池台。
何时石门路，
重有金樽开。
秋波落泗水，
海色明徂徕。
飞蓬各自远，
且尽手中杯。

# Send-off of Fu Tu at Stone Gate, East Lu

After you left me for some time,
All the riverside towers I climb.
When by Stone Gate can we gather
And drain our gold cups together?
All autumn waters roll to sheen;
The Tsulai Mountains sheen sea-green.
Like thistledown, blown down and up,
Why not raise and finish our cup?

* Fu Tu: Fu Tu (A.D. 712 – A.D. 770), a down-to-earth realistic poet in the Tang dynasty, one of the greatest poets in the history, regarded as "Saint of Poetry" to go with "God of Poetry", i.e., Pai Li, a romantic knight-errant, a good friend of Fu Tu's. As two polarities, Fu Tu was more a Confucian, cerebral, moral, and socially-engaged, and Pai Li more a Wordist, intuitive, amoral, and detached.
* the Tsulai Mountains: 20 kilometers from today's Yanchow, Shantung Province.

# 鲁郡尧祠送张十四游河北

猛虎伏尺草，
虽藏难蔽身。
有如张公子，
肮脏在风尘。
岂无横腰剑，
屈彼淮阴人。
击筑向北燕，
燕歌易水滨。
归来泰山上，
当与尔为邻。

## Seeing Off Chang Fourteen to Tour North of the River at Mound's Shrine in the County of Lu

The tiger lurking in grass low
All its stripes, back and tail, does show.
Like Childe of the Chang's with us here,
Through the dustly world he does peer.
Don't have a sword worn on your waist,
Like Hsin Han in Huaishade debased?
In North Yan the *quin* you will play
And by the Change sing a Yan lay.
Come back to Mt. Arch when you can,
I'll be your neighbor good, dear man.

* Mound's Shrine: 2.5 kilometers from today's Linfen, Shanhsi Province.
* tiger: a large carnivorous feline mammal of Asia, with vertical black wavy stripes on a tawny body and black bars or rings on the limbs and tail, praised as king of all animals.
* Hsin Han: a founding commander of the Han regime. He had been poor and shown a good endurance of humiliation. Once a young man made fun of him and forced him to crawl through his legs, and Han did so without changing his expression. When he was not appreciated in pursuit of an official career or good at doing business, Han used to rely on an elder laundry woman who pitied him and gave him food without expectation of a return.
* Huaishade: the birthplace of Hsin Han, a founding commander of Han.
* North Yan: the State of Yan (1044 B.C.- 222 B.C.), located approximately in today's Chi County, Tientsin, a state enfeoffed to Lord Shao when King Martial conquered King Chow of Shang.
* *quin*: an ancient Chinese musical instrument with five strings like a Quinton, played by striking with a bamboo node, producing a very moving and tragic sound.
* the Change: referring to the River Change, by which Chingk'e bid farewell to his lord and friend, and set off for his mission.
* Mt. Arch: one of the Five Mountains in China, located in Shantung Province, along with Mt. Ever in Shanhsi, Mt. Scale in Hunan, Mt. Flora in Sha'anhsi, and Mt. Tower in Honan. Mt. Arch is the most sacred of the five, because 72 sovereigns in prehistoric China made sacrifices to the god of the mountain and 12 emperors made sacrifices from the Ch'in dynasty to the Ch'ing dynasty, clearly recorded in history books.

# 杭州送裴大泽赴庐州长史

西江天柱远，
东越海门深。
去割慈亲恋，
行忧报国心。
好风吹落日，
流水引长吟。
五月披裘者，
应知不取金。

# Seeing Off Tatse P'ei in Hangchow to His Secretary Post in Lodge

Mt. Post sees the West River flow
To Seagate in East Yüeh like so.
From dear ones it is hard to part;
To serve the state does urge your heart.
The wind to the setting sun blows;
The river sings to you and flows.
The woodcutter in the fifth moon
Works not for gold but gives a boon.

* Lodge: a prefecture in the T'ang dynasty, what is now Hofei, the capital of Anhui Province.
* Mt. Post: in Lodge Prefecture in T'ang dynasty, that is today's Hofei, Anhui Province.
* Seagate: 37.5 kilometers from Jenho County.

# 灞陵行送别

送君灞陵亭，
灞水流浩浩。
上有无花之古树，
下有伤心之春草。
我向秦人问路歧，
云是王粲南登之古道。
古道连绵走西京，
紫阙落日浮云生。
正当今夕断肠处，
骊歌愁绝不忍听。

# Farewell at Paridge Kiosk

At Paridge Kiosk I fare you well,
The Pa River flows on to swell.
Above, the trees stand, flowerless and so old;
Below, the grass sways up woes manifold.
I ask a traveler: "Where shall I go, pray?"
He replies: Ts'an Wang used to take that southward old way.
The old way zigzags to Capital west,
Where the palace is with black clouds depressed.
While I'm so worried by the setting sun,
A parting song hurts me, the lonely one

* Paridge: the ancient name of Yüehshine, where Emperor Civil of Han was buried.
* Ts'an Wang: a brilliant litterateur with high reputation in the late Eastern Han dynasty.
* the Pa River: 15 kilometers from Long Peace, the capital of T'ang.

## 送贺监归四明应制

久辞荣禄遂初衣,
曾向长生说息机。
真诀自从茅氏得,
恩波宁阻洞庭归。
瑶台含雾星辰满,
仙峤浮空岛屿微。
借问欲栖珠树鹤,
何年却向帝城飞。

## Seeing Off Chihchang Ho to Mt. Four Bright, a Poem Composed by an Imperial Order

To go back to the folks, you have resigned;
Saying to live long one needs a free mind.
From Mister Mao you've got the long-life knack;
For all His grace, to Cavehall you'll go back.
The Jade Dais in mist greets stars on high;
The Fairy Peaks amid isles reach the sky.
You're going to perch on the pearl tree, crane.
When would you fly to Capital again?

\* Chihchang Ho: Chihchang Ho (A.D. 659 - A.D. 744), Pai Li's friend, an imperial tutor, a jovial courtier, a renowned poet and calligraphist, one of the Eight Immortals of the Wine Cup. He introduced Pai Li to Emperor Deepsire. At 86, he requested leave to return to his home in Shaohsing to become a Wordist monk and rose to Heaven then and there.

\* Mister Mao: a Wordist who was said to become immortal in legends.

- * Cavehall: a big lake in Hunan Province.
- * Jade Dais: indicating the place where immortals dwell.
- * the Fairy Mound: an imaginary place fairies dwell.
- * pearl tree: an immortal tree in Chinese mythology and legend, sometimes referring to a beautiful tree or a tree capped with snow, and a metaphor for a handsome talent.
- * crane: one of a family of large, long-necked, long-legged, heronlike birds allied to the rails, having pure white plumage, a symbol of integrity and longevity in Chinese culture, only second to the phoenix in cultural importance.

## 送窦司马贬宜春

天马白银鞍，
亲承明主欢。
斗鸡金宫里，
射雁碧云端。
堂上罗中贵，
歌钟清夜阑。
何言谪南国，
拂剑坐长叹。
赵璧为谁点，
隋珠枉被弹。
圣朝多雨露，
莫厌此行难。

## Seeing Off Commander Tou Exiled to Fitspring

Your horse with silver saddle on,
The lord's grace and favor you won.
At court you played, seeing cocks fight;
Out you shot down wild geese in flight.
In splendid halls you had much fun,
Plays did not stop till night was gone.
To South you're exiled, so alone;
A-stroking your sword, you do moan.
Which fly has stained Chao's Jade with dirt?
What curse has wronged Sui's Pearl so hurt?

His Majesty shines like the sun;
Don't hate into mud you have run.

* Fitspring: referring to Echun if transliterated.
* seeing cocks fight: referring to the game of cockfighting or cockfight. Cockfighting has a long history in China, a main recreational activity all through history. The earliest cockfighting in China recorded in *Historical Records* was in 770 B.C.
* wild goose: an undomesticated goose that is caring and responsible, taken as a symbol of benevolence, righteousness, good manner, wisdom, and faith in Chinese culture.
* Chao's Jade: referring to the jade found by Ho Pien.
* Sui's Pearl: a precious pearl in history. Lord Sui saved an injured snake on his way to Ch'i. Not long after, he got a pearl in return.

# 送羽林陶将军

将军出使拥楼船，
江上旌旗拂紫烟。
万里横戈探虎穴，
三杯拔剑舞龙泉。
莫道词人无胆气，
临行将赠绕朝鞭。

## To T'ao, General of Armed Escort

General T'ao the warship does command;
The flags flow to sweep off mist aboard.
You'll explore tiger dens across the land;
And after three cups of wine play your sword.
Don't you say a poet like me is not brave;
Leaving now, I'll give you a whip to wave.

* General T'ao: unidentified in this poem.
* tiger: a large carnivorous feline mammal of Asia, with vertical black wavy stripes on a tawny body and black bars or rings on the limbs and tail, praised as king of all animals.
* a whip to wave: In 615 B.C., the king of the State of Chin succeeded in reclaiming through espionage Shi Hui who had defected to Ch'in. When Shi Hui was leaving, a Ch'in minister gave Shi Hui a whip, saying: "It's a pity that my advice was not taken by our Lord, but don't you think I have not seen through your trick." A whip to wave has since been used as a token of words given at parting.

# 送程刘二侍郎兼独孤判官赴安西幕府

安西幕府多材雄，
喧喧惟道三数公。
绣衣貂裘明积雪，
飞书走檄如飘风。
朝辞明主出紫宫，
银鞍送别金城空。
天外飞霜下葱海，
火旗云马生光彩。
胡塞清尘几日归，
汉家草绿遥相待。

# Seeing Off Ministers Ch'eng and Liu to Be Aides in Pacified West Tent Office

In West Tent Office heroes rise to be;
The most renowned of all are but you three.
Your embroidered marten coat outshines snow;
Your writing brush runs along like a blow.
You take leave of Purple Palace at dawn;
Now your horse's gone, it's an empty town.
Out there frost glistens on the Leekhill sand;
Fine horses fly and glow, radiantly grand.
The desert will see peace and green quell dust;
When grass grows lush, I'll wait for you, I must.

* Pacified West: a military and political institution or a protectorate set up in the town of

Link River in Turpan in A.D. 640 to pacify and govern the west regions of China.
* West Tent Office: Pacified West Tent Office, referring to the protectorate first based in Link River in A.D. 640 and then moved to Kuci (Kuqa) in A.D. 648, governing four towns in the western regions of China, covering an area as far as Persian Bay and much of today's New Land (Hsinchiang) Autonomous Region.
* marten: a weasel-like fur-bearing carnivorous animal (genus *Martes*) having arboreal habits as the pine marten and the large sturdy fisher marten; also the fur of a marten used for the making of expensive clothing.
* writing brush: any of various writing brushes or called Chinese brush, widely used for writing or painting, invented or renovated by Tien Meng (259 B.C.- 210 B.C.), a general in the Ch'in dynasty.
* Purple Palace: referring to the royal palace. The color purple symbolizes royal power or dignity in China as well as in the west.
* the Leekhill sand: the desert near the Leekhill on the Pamirs, where a post was stationed by West Tent Office. The hill got its name because the hill was lush with wild leek.

## 送侄良携二妓赴会稽，戏有此赠

携妓东山去，
春光半道催。
遥看若桃李，
双入镜中开。

## Seeing Off Liang, My Nephew to Mt. Summit with Two Singers, a Poem for Fun

Two belles you take in the East Hills;
Half way there, the spring spirit trills.
There seems a peach and here a plum;
Into your mirror they both come.

* Mt. Summit: referring to the K'uaichi Mountains in present-day Chechiang Province, where Worm convened a summit attended by vassal lords, hence the name.
* the East Hills: 27.5 kilometers southwest of Shangyü County, Shaohsing, a place for reclusion, where An Hsieh (A.D. 320 – A.D. 385), a statesman and litterateur with high reputation, lived with ease and kept declining official positions until he was in his forties. It is often used as a metaphor for reclusion.
* peach: any of the plant (*Prunus Percica*), bearing a fleshy, juicy, edible drupe, cultivated in many varieties in temperate zones considered sacred in China, a symbol of romance, prosperity and longevity.
* plum: a kind of plant or the edible purple drupaceous fruit of the plant which is any one of various trees of the genus *Prunus*, cultivated in temperate zones.

## 送贺宾客归越

镜湖流水漾清波，
狂客归舟逸兴多。
山阴道士如相见，
应写黄庭换白鹅。

## Seeing Off Chihchang Ho Back to Yüeh

Lake Mirror ripples to ripples flows on,
You mad ones row back, having had much fun.
If you meet the Wordist, verse you may write
So to exchange like Wang for a goose white.

* Chihchang Ho: Chihchang Ho (A.D. 659 – A.D. 744), a jovial courtier, renowned poet and calligrapher in the T'ang dynasty, who acclaimed Pai Li as Fallen Immortal to the public and introduced him to Emperor Deepsire.
* Lake Mirror: a large reservoir built in the Han dynasty, higher than the fields and the fields higher than the sea, 310 li in circumference.
* Wordist: one who believes in or professes belief of Wordism, the doctrines declared by Laocius (571 B.C.– 471 B.C.).
* Wang: referring to Hsichih Wang (A.D. 303 – A.D. 379), highborn calligrapher in the Eastern Chin dynasty, regarded as the Sage of Handwriting. Wang adored a group of geese raised by a Wordist and wrote a verse in exchange for the geese.
* goose: one of a subfamily (*Anserinae*) of wild or domesticated web-footed birds larger than ducks and smaller than swans, usually a sign of good luck because of its red protruding head.

# 送张遥之寿阳幕府

寿阳信天险，
天险横荆关。
苻坚百万众，
遥阻八公山。
不假筑长城，
大贤在其间。
战夫若熊虎，
破敌有馀闲。
张子勇且英，
少轻卫霍屑。
投躯紫髯将，
千里望风颜。
勖尔效才略，
功成衣锦还。

# Seeing Off Yao Chang to Lifeshine Tent Office

Lifeshine's such a strategic place,
A place that does Bramble Pass brace.
Chien Fu, with troops a million strong,
Was checked at Eight Lords, thereamong.
There're no such things as the Great Wall;
A man so great can defend all.
If mad like a tiger and bear,
One can kill all, with vim to spare.

Chang, buddy, brave, handsome and wise,
Even Wei and Huo you despise.
General Purple Beard you'll serve well;
The foes will flee away pell-mell.
May you, our hero, do your best,
And come back home, in brocade dressed.

* Lifeshine: referring to Shouyang if transliterated, located in present-day Anhui.
* Bramble Pass: referring to the Bramble Mountain, a dangerous passway.
* Chien Fu: Chien Fu (A.D. 338 - A.D. 385), a Lord of Fore-Ch'in in the Sixteen States period. During his reign, the state was booming in economy and military forces. Fu wiped out several states in the north and unified the northern lands, but was defeated by An Hsieh, commander of the Eastern Chin, when Fu sent his troops to the south.
* Eight Lords: referring to a mountain in Anhui.
* A man so great: referring to An Hsieh (A.D. 320 - A.D. 385), a statesman and renowned scholar in the Eastern Chin dynasty.
* the Great Wall: usually called Ten-thousand-li Great Wall, a giant project undertaken in different periods of Chinese history to defend China from northern nomadic invasions, mostly first built in the Ch'in dynasty, third century B.C., by forced labour including political prisoners.
* Wei: referring to Ch'ing Wei (? - 106 B.C.), a renowned commander in the Western Han dynasty.
* Huo: referring to Swift Huo (140 B.C.- 117 B.C.), a renowned general, prominent strategist and patriotic hero in the Han dynasty. He made his first show at 17, leading 800 fierce cavalrymen to penetrate into enemy lines and defeat the Huns. Huo fought against the Huns in three major wars and each time returned with victory. He died of illness at 24, leaving his achievements as one of the highest glories for Chinese military commanders.
* General Purple Beard: referring to any brave general.
* come back home, in brocade dressed: an allusion to Overlord Hsiang's saying of going back home in triumph. When Overlord Hsiang captured Allshine, he was advised to stay and claim throne, but looking at the ruins of Ch'in's palace, a sign of his success, he replied: "When rich and powerful, if one does not go back home, it is like going in brocade at night. Who knows him?"

## 送裴十八图南归嵩山二首
## Seeing Off T'unan P'ei Back South to Mt. Tower, Two Poems

### 其 一

何处可为别，
长安青绮门。
胡姬招素手，
延客醉金樽。
临当上马时，
我独与君言。
风吹芳兰折，
日没鸟雀喧。
举手指飞鸿，
此情难具论。
同归无早晚，
颍水有清源。

### No. 1

Where shall I fare you well, my mate?
At Capital's Green Damask Gate.
Hun girls wave their hand to cheer up
And invite us to drink a cup.
Now on your horse, you'll soon depart;
I've one word for you from my heart.
A wind blows and orchids give in;
The sun set, one hears sparrows' din.

Remember the flight of wild geese?
But I'm so caged, so ill at ease.
Back to nature we both will go;
Where we'll see the Ying clearly flow.

* Mt. Tower: located in the west of present-day Honan Province, one of the Five Sacred Mountains in Chinese culture.
* Hun girls: foreign girls from west or north of China, often selling wine in wine shops in the T'ang dynasty, featured with a high nose, charming eyes and brimming with enthusiasm and ardor.
* Green Damask Gate: the southernmost gate of Long Peace.
* orchid: a terrestrial or epiphytic monocotyledonous plant having thickened bulbous roots and often very showy distinctive flowers, one of the four most important floral images in Chinese literature, which are wintersweet, orchid, bamboo and chrysanthemum.
* sparrow: a small, plain-colored passerine bird related to the finches, grosbeaks and buntings, a very common bird in China, a symbol of insignificance.
* the flight of wild geese: the flag decorated with wild geese in flight.
* the Ying: referring to the River Ying, a river derived from Mt. Tower, 620 kilometers long, as is the biggest branch of the Huai River. The River Ying has been regarded as one of the origins of Chinese culture.

## 其 二

君思颖水绿，
忽复归嵩岑。
归时莫洗耳，
为我洗其心。
洗心得真情，
洗耳徒买名。
谢公终一起，
相与济苍生。

## No. 2

You may miss the Ying River blue,
As back to Tower you start to go.
Don't wash your ears in Freedom's way,
But do cleanse your mind if you may.
Your mind cleansed, you fulfil your aim;
Your ears washed, you build on your fame.
Lord Hsieh will rise once more one day;
To save the world, he'll make his way.

* the Ying River: a river derived from Mt. Tower, looking yellow with sand flowing with currents like the Yellow River. The River Ying has been regarded as one of the origins of Chinese culture.
* Freedom: Yu Hsu, a precedent of Wordists in the age of Mound and Hibiscus. When Mound wanted to offer his throne to Freedom, the latter regarded it as a shame and went to a river to wash his ears because he thought the offer had dirtied his ears.
* Tower: referring to Mt. Tower, located in the west of present-day Honan Province, one of the Five Mountains in Chinese culture.
* Your ears washed: indicating Freedom, that is, Yu Hsu if transliterated, a hermit of

talent. He washed his ears at the River Ying as soon as he heard that Mound intended to abdicate his throne to him.

* Lord Hsieh: referring to An Hsieh (A.D. 320 - A.D. 385), a statesman and renowned scholar in the Eastern Chin dynasty. He once lived in seclusion and went back to defend the country when Chien Fu sent troops to conquer the Eastern Chin.

## 同王昌龄送族弟襄归桂阳二首

## Seeing Off My Cousin Hsiang Li Back to Cassiashine with Ch'angling Wang, Two Poems

### 其 一

秦地见碧草，
楚谣对清樽。
把酒尔何思，
鹧鸪啼南园。
余欲罗浮隐，
犹怀明主恩。
跨踏紫宫恋，
孤负沧洲言。
终然无心云，
海上同飞翻。
相期乃不浅，
幽桂有芳根。

### No. 1

Ch'in Land now sees all grass grow up;
A Ch'u rhyme's sung to our clear cup.
You do not drink but think, o why?
In southern park some partridges cry.
I'd climb La Phu, from dust away;
But Lord's kindness I should repay.
The court sees me pace to and fro;

Now back to Nature I can't go!
But after all, I'm a cloud free,
I will fly with you o'er the sea.
Perhaps, before long we will meet,
As fragrant laurels have roots sweet.

* Cassiashine: referring to Kuiyang if transliterated, a county in present-day Ch'enchow, Hunan Province.
* Ch'angling Wang: Ch'angling Wang (A.D. 698 - A.D. 757), a poet in the T'ang dynasty, especially good at writing poems about the frontier.
* Ch'in: the Ch'in State or the State of Ch'in (905 B.C - 206 B.C.), enfeoffed as a dependency of Chough by King Piety of Chough in 905 B.C. and enfeoffed as a vassal state by King Peace of Chough in 770 B.C. In the ten years from 230 B.C. to 221 B.C., Ch'in wiped out the other six powers and became the first unified regime of China, i.e. the Ch'in Empire.
* Ch'u: a vassal state of Chough, one of the powers in the Warring States period, conquered and annexed by Ch'in in 223 B.C.
* partridge: a kind of small, plump-bodied gallinaceous game bird, having white spots on the chest, a symbol of lovesickness in Chinese culture, as it utters a cry sounding like: "bro-bro, no-go-go".
* La Phu: an attractive mountain in Kuangtung where Surge Ko, a hermit in the Chin dynasty, used to live in seclusion.

## 其 二

尔家何在潇湘川，
青莎白石长沙边。
昨梦江花照江日，
几枝正发东窗前。
觉来欲往心悠然，
魂随越鸟飞南天。
秦云连山海相接，
桂水横烟不可涉。
送君此去令人愁，
风帆茫茫隔河洲。
春潭琼草绿可折，
西寄长安明月楼。

## No. 2

The Hsiao and the Hsiang are where you abide;
With green flatsedge and white boulders beside.
You dreamed of sunlit blooms ashore last night;
Before East Window some sprays blew so bright.
When you woke up, your heart would jump to fly,
Fly with the migrant birds across the south sky.
The mountains and seas linked by clouds from west,
You couldn't cross the Cassia with fog pressed.
While faring you well, I feel my heart fail;
Beyond the shoal the mist veils all your sail.
The fair grass by Spring Pool you can deflower;
Send it west to Long Peace, to my Moon Tower.

* The Hsiao and the Hsiang: referring to two rivers in today's Hunan Province, the River Hsiao and the River Hsiang, hence implying the area covering Hunan.
* flatsedge: any herb of *Cyperus rotundus*, growing in wet places or marshes.
* the Cassia: or the Kui if transliterated, a river that originates from Hunan Province and flows to Kuilin, implying Kuilin, a picturesque city in present-day Kuanghsi Province.
* Long Peace: referring to Ch'ang'an if transliterated, the metropolis of gold, the capital of the T'ang, the largest walled city ever built by man and a cosmopolis of world religions, Buddhism, Confucianism, Wordism, Nestorianism, Zoroastrianism, and even Islamism represented by Saracens. It was the wonder of the age that reached the pinnacle of brilliance in Emperor Deepsire's reign: The main castle with its nine-fold gates, the thirty-six imperial palaces, pillars of gold, innumerable mansions and villas of noblemen, the broad avenues thronged with motley crowds of townsfolk, gallants on horseback, and mandarin cars drawn by yokes of black oxen, countless houses of pleasure, which opened their doors by night all made this city a kaleidoscope of miracles.

## 送外甥郑灌从军三首

## Seeing Off My Nephew Kuan Cheng to Join the Army, Three Poems

### 其 一

六博争雄好彩来，
金盘一掷万人开。
丈夫赌命报天子，
当斩胡头衣锦回。

### No. 1

To win six-chessmate game, one his luck tries;
When chips are placed, to rush everyone vies.
A good man should repay his Lord instead;
He'd come back in triumph with a Hun's head.

* six-chessmates game: an ancient game, popular in the Chough dynasty, especially the Warring States period, played by two players, each having six chessmates, one of which is owl and the other five goers. A move is determined by a chopstick thrown at the target. It has been believed to be the progenitor of chess, Chinese chess, international chess, shogi and so on.
* Hun: war-like nomadic peoples occupying vast regions from Mongolia to Central Asia in Chinese history, especially during the Han dynasty. They were a headache and a constant menace on China's western and northern borders.

## 其 二

丈八蛇矛出陇西，
弯弧拂箭白猿啼。
破胡必用龙韬策，
积甲应将熊耳齐。

## No. 2

West Bulge sees lance spears march along and out;
At arrow and bow the white monkeys shout.
*Six Arts* must be used to wipe out Huns clear;
Their weapons piled up will top Mt. Bear's Ear.

* West Bulge: Lunghsi if transliterated, name of a shire in the Warring States period and the T'ang dynasty, covering today's Lanchow, West Buldge and Lint'ao.
* lance spear: an ancient weapon about three meters long and its spearhead about 26 centimeters long, made of pattern steel.
* *Six Arts*: a book on the art of war written by Great Grand, an influential strategist and statesman who helped establish the Western Chough and exerted a profound influence on the political and military affairs of ancient China.
* Hun: a nationality that has the same origin as Chinese. In approximately 16th century B.C., a branch of the Hsia family fled to the north and annexed other tribes, hence the formation of the Hun nationality.
* Their weapons piled up will top Mt. Bear's Ear: Mt. Bear is an offset of Ch'in Ridge, located in the west of today's Honan Province. In the beginning of the Eastern Han dynasty, Red Brows surrendered to Hsiu Liu, the new emperor, and their abandoned weapons were piled east of Fitshine (Eyang), as high as Mt. Bear's Ear nearby.

## 其 三

月蚀西方破敌时，
及瓜归日未应迟。
斩胡血变黄河水，
枭首当悬白鹊旗。

## No. 3

Moon eclipsed in the west, foes you will wipe,
And you should come back when melons are ripe.
When the River flows with Huns' blood to slop,
Their heads will be hung on magpie flags' top.

* the moon: the planet of the earth, which appears at night and gives off shining silvery light, an image of purity and solitude in Chinese culture.
* melon: a trailing plant of the gourd family, or its fruit. There are two genera, the muskmelon and the watermelon, each with numerous varieties, growing in both tropical and temperate zones.
* the River: referring to the Yellow River.
* Hun: a nomadic people in north and west of China or enemy in general though they shared the same blood as Chinese.
* magpie flag: a flag decorated with a white magpie figure.

## 送于十八应四子举落第还嵩山

吾祖吹橐籥，
天人信森罗。
归根复太素，
群动熙元和。
炎炎四真人，
摛辩若涛波。
交流无时寂，
杨墨日成科。
夫子闻洛诵，
夸才才固多。
为金好踊跃，
久客方蹉跎。
道可束卖之，
五宝溢山河。
劝君还嵩丘，
开酌盼庭柯。
三花如未落，
乘兴一来过。

## Seeing Off Yü Eighteen to Mt. Tower After He Failed Grand Test

My sire, the bellows worked he;
Many immortals there must be.
All on earth reduced to the One,
Many have come out of the None.

The four true men enjoying fame

Argued, refuted, like aflame.

Not a single day did they stop;

Yang and Sir Ink came to the top.

Confucius who did chant and read

Was praised as a talent indeed.

Moyeh's swords were always the best;

Unrecognized, he felt depressed.

The Word cannot be wholesale sold,

A treasure, real silver and gold.

Go back to Mt. Tower, go back pray,

Cup held, viewing a flowering spray.

If pattra flowers still bloom their way,

On an impulse I'll come to stay.

* Mt. Tower: located in the west of present-day Honan Province, one of the Five Mountains in Chinese culture. It is one of the five sanctuaries of Wordism, and the abode of God of Mt. Tower worshipped by Han Chinese, with an area of 450 square kilometers, consisting of Mt. Greatroom and Mt. Smallroom, having 72 peaks, 350 meters above sea level at the lowest and 1,512 meters at the highest.
* my sire: referring to Laocius, one of the most influential philosophers of Wordism in China, the proponent of quietism. Laocius wrote all his wisdom into a single book of about five thousand words, which came to be known as *The World and the World*.
* the four true men: referring to Sir Lush, Sir Civil, Sir Line and Mulberry Vitex, four famous Wordists in the Warring States period.
* Yang: referring to Chu Yang (395 B.C.- 335 B.C.), a great philosopher in the Warring States period, who advocated the thoughts of Laocius and Sir Lush.
* Sir Ink: Sir Ink (cir. 476 B.C.- 390 B.C.), a philosopher, educator, scientist, martial strategist in the late Spring and Autumn period and the early Warring States period, and the founder of Inkism which was regarded as one of the two most prestigious schools along with Confucianism.
* Confucius: Confucius (551 B.C.- 479 B.C.) was a renowned thinker, educator and statesman in the Spring and Autumn period, born in the State of Lu, and as the founder of Confucianism, has exerted profound influence on Chinese culture.

* Moyeh: one of two renowned ancient swordsmen, i.e., Kanchiang and Moyeh.
* pattra: meaning leaf in Sanskrit, on which Buddhist sutra were written, often called pattra-leaf scriptures.

# 送　　别

寻阳五溪水，
沿洄直入巫山里。
胜境由来人共传，
君到南中自称美。
送君别有八月秋，
飒飒芦花复益愁。
云帆望远不相见，
日暮长江空自流。

# Good-bye

In Bankshine County there are five rills,
Which zigzag and zigzag to the Witch Hills.
This wonderful place, as e'er, all people praise;
When you're there, South Land all its charm displays.
It's autumn now while I bid you good-bye;
Reed catkins against a sough make me sigh.
As you sail, I can't see you any more;
At dusk, the Long River flows to my sore.

* Bankshine: an ancient name of present-day Chiuchiang, Chianghsi Province.
* the Witch Hills: referring to Mt. Witch, a mythical and religious mountain, which was thought to be a range of mountains in Sha'anhsi.
* catkin: a deciduous scaly spike of flowers, as in the willow, an image of helpless drifting or wandering in Chinese literature.
* the Long River: the longest river in China, originating from the T'angkula Mountains on Tibet Plateau, flowing through 11 provincial areas, more than 6,300 kilometers long, the third longest river in the world.

## 送族弟绾从军安西

汉家兵马乘北风,
鼓行而西破犬戎。
尔随汉将出门去,
剪虏若草收奇功。
君王按剑望边色,
旄头已落胡天空。
匈奴系颈数应尽,
明年应入蒲萄宫。

## Seeing Off My Cousin Kuan to Join the Army in Pacified West

The troops and chariots run as north wind blows;
The drum boosts soldiers to wipe out Hun foes.
With T'ang's general out of the gate you run;
The foes cut like grass, your war will be won.
Hand on sword, the Lord to the front does peer;
The Pleiades from the Huns' sky disappear.
The Hun foes will have tried their last resort;
Next year you'll gallop back to please the court.

* Pacified West: Pacified West Tent Office, the protectorate that was first based in Link River in A.D. 640 and then moved to Kuci (Kuqa) in A.D. 648, governing four towns in the western regions of China, covering an area as far as Persian Bay and much of today's New Land (Hsinchiang) Autonomous Region.
* the Pleiades: a loose cluster of many hundred stars in the constellation of Taurus, six of which are visible to ordinary sight.

* Hun: nomadic Asian people from north and west, a persistent enemy of China, who had no trade but battle and carnage, no fields or plough lands but only wastes where white bones lay scattered over yellow sands.

## 送梁公昌从信安北征

入幕推英选，
捐书事远戎。
高谈百战术，
郁作万夫雄。
起舞莲花剑，
行歌明月弓。
将飞天地阵，
兵出塞垣通。
祖席留丹景，
征麾拂彩虹。
旋应献凯入，
麟阁仁深功。

## Seeing Off Ch'ang Liang to North Expedition Under Prince of Real Peace

You are chosen as you're the best;
Out of your study, you'll fight west.
The arts of war you talk about,
And will fight all, so brave and stout.
You dance while Lotus Sword you play;
You sing as Crescent Bow you sway.
As general, you've planned the war;
All thru the pass your men will pour.
I will make this feast the best view,
Your armor touched with rainbow hue.

Good news will rush in like a tide,
And your name will be carved with pride

* Prince of Real Peace: Ee Li (? – A.D. 743), the founding emperor Shimin Li's third son.

# 送白利从金吾董将军西征

西羌延国讨，
白起佐军威。
剑决浮云气，
弓弯明月辉。
马行边草绿，
旌卷曙霜飞。
抗手凛相顾，
寒风生铁衣。

## Seeing Off Li Pai to the West Expedition Under General Tung of the Garrison

Our T'ang Empire will Tibet fight,
Son of the Pai's, you'll show your might.
Your sword will cut the airs of the foe,
While the moon shines over your bow.
Your horse across green runs ahead;
The frosty flags at daybreak spread.
The soldiers each other do accost;
A wind dyes their armor with frost.

* Tibet: a former theocracy of Central Asia, of Chiang origin. Chinese descended from Old Chiang about 6,000 years ago. In this case Chiang, Tibetans and Chinese have the same origin.
* the Pai's: referring to White Rise (Ch'i Pai if transliterated) (? - 257 B.C.), more formally called Rise Lordson, a representative military strategist in the Warring States period, who helped the State of Ch'in greatly in the unification of China.

\* the moon: the celestial body that revolves around the earth from west to east, which appears at night and gives off shining silvery light, an image of purity and solitude in Chinese culture.

## 送张秀才从军

六驳食猛虎，
耻从驽马群。
一朝长鸣去，
矫若龙行云。
壮士怀远略，
志存解世纷。
周粟犹不顾，
齐珪安肯分。
抱剑辞高堂，
将投霍冠军。
长策扫河洛，
宁亲归汝坟。
当令千古后，
麟阁著奇勋。

## Seeing Off Chang, a Showcharm, to Join the Army

The unicorn eats tigers, its game;
To be with nags it feels the shame.
Today you leave with a long cry,
Like a dragon that does fly high.
Aimed high, strong willed, you look afar,
Settling world troubles as they are.
Chough's millet you would deny;
How could you vain posts occupy?

To your parents farewell you say,
And with General Ts'ui you'll stay.
With tactics rebels you'll wipe smack
And then to hometown you'll come back.
You'll be well remembered for e'er;
Your name is carved with pride to flare.

* showcharm: a talent recommended for official use through civil-service examinations or a well-learned person in ancient China.
* unicorn: a fabulous deer-like animal with one horn, a symbol of saintliness and divinity in Chinese culture. Confucius lamented the death of a unicorn captured and hence stopped compiling *The Spring and Autumn Annals* and died before long.
* tiger: a large ferocious carnivorous feline mammal of Asia, with bright spotlight-like eyes, sharp teeth, vertical black wavy stripes on a tawny body and black bars or rings on the limbs and tail, praised as king of all animals.
* nag: an old or inferior horse, a metaphor for a worthless person.
* Chough's millet you would deny: implying high moral integrity by borrowing the story of Bowone and Straightthree, childes in the late Shang dynasty. As they failed to admonish King Martial of Chough, Bowone and Straightthree left King Chough and refused to take crops reaped under the reign of Chough. They lived on fungi on Mt. Firstshine and starved to death in the end.

## 送崔度还吴度故人礼部员外国辅之子

幽燕沙雪地，
万里尽黄云。
朝吹归秋雁，
南飞日几群。
中有孤凤雏，
哀鸣九天闻。
我乃重此鸟，
彩章五色分。
胡为杂凡禽，
雏鹜轻贱君。
举手捧尔足，
疾心若火焚。
拂羽泪满面，
送之吴江濆。
去影忽不见，
踌躇日将嚑。

## Seeing Off Tu Ts'ui Back to Wu, Who Is a Son of My Friend, Kuofu Ts'ui, a Councillor of the Ministry of Rites

In Dim Yan there flies snow and sand;
A dust storm sweeps across the land.
The autumn dawn hears wild geese cry;
Each day a few flights southward fly.
A phoenix strays there, and the bird

Whines high above, so sad as heard.
This bird I treasure very much;
Its plumes give off a gleam as such.
How can it flock with fowls so vain,
Which this noble bird all disdain.
I hold your feet and do them raise;
My heart's so hot, as if ablaze.
Your plumes I stroke, tears dripping down:
You'll fly south to your hometown.
Your shadow fleets, suddenly gone,
I pace and face the setting sun.

* Dim Yan: the State of Yan or northern area of China in general.
* wild goose: an undomesticated goose that is caring and responsible, taken as a symbol of benevolence, righteousness, good manner, wisdom and faith in Chinese culture.
* phoenix: the king of all birds, an auspicious sign in Chinese civilization. In Egyptian mythology it is a legendary bird of great beauty, unique of its kind, which was supposed to live five or six hundred years before consuming itself by fire, rising again from its ashes to live through another cycle, a symbol of immortality. In Chinese mythology, the phoenix is the most beautiful bird that only perches on phoenix trees, i.e. firmiana, only eats firmiana fruit, and only drinks sweet spring water, and this mythic bird appears only in times of peace and sagacious rule.
* fowls: the common domestic cocks, hens, or chickens, poultry in general. The domestication of the fowl in China was begun more than 5,000 years ago according to archaeological finds.

## 送祝八之江东，赋得浣纱石

西施越溪女，
明艳光云海。
未入吴王宫殿时，
浣纱古石今犹在。
桃李新开映古查，
菖蒲犹短出平沙。
昔时红粉照流水，
今日青苔覆落花。
君去西秦适东越，
碧山青江几超忽。
若到天涯思故人，
浣纱石上窥明月。

## Seeing Off Tsu Eight to the East, a Verse of Washing Stone

West Maid, a washer on Yüeh's Stream
To clouds and seas did shine her gleam.
She entered King of Wu's palace that year;
The stone on which she washed yarns still lies here.
The peaches bloom to the old raft astrand;
The bulrushes grow just out of the sand.
Then her powder and rouge did the flow gloss;
Now her bloom has fallen to the green moss.
Now leaving Capital, in Yüeh you'll be;
The green hills and blue rivers there fret me.

> I might join you at the end of the sky;
> On Washing Stone we'll view the moon on high.

* West Maid: once a laundry lady in the State of Yüeh which was then a tributary to the State of Wu. Because of her beauty, West Maid was selected to be trained in Yüeh's palace, and sent to the King of Wu as a spy. She quickly won the king's affection, making him indulged in her charm. As a result, the State of Wu waned and perished.
* peach: any tree of the genus *Prunus Percica*, blooming brilliantly and bearing fruit, a fleshy, juicy, edible drupe.
* bulrush: a tall, rushlike plant growing in damp ground or water, such as the tall sedge.
* moss: a tiny, delicate green bryophytic plant growing on damp decaying wood, wet ground, humid rocks or trees, producing capsules which open by an operculum and contain spores. Under a poet's writing brush, it may arouse a poetic feeling or imagination.
* Capital: Long Peace or Ch'ang'an if transliterated, the capital of the T'ang Empire, a cosmopolis with 1,000,000 inhabitants, the largest walled city ever built by man, the center of world religions, Buddhism, Confucianism, Wordism, Nestorianism, Zoroastrianism, and even Islamism represented by Saracens, and the center of education—There were colleges of various grades and special institutes for calligraphy, arithmetic, music, astronomy and so on.
* Washing Stone: the stone on which West Maid washed yarn.

# 送侯十一

朱亥已击晋，
侯嬴尚隐身。
时无魏公子，
岂贵抱关人。
余亦不火食，
游梁同在陈。
空馀湛卢剑，
赠尔托交亲。

## Seeing Off Hou Eleven

When Chu attacked General Pi Chin,
Ying Hou was a hermit therein.
There's no Prince of Way debonair;
Who will respect Hou, who will care?
I have no warm food, no food left,
In Liang like him in Ch'en, bereft.
I'll give you this sword and its glare,
A gift for the best man, whoe'er.

* Chu: referring to Hai Chu, a butcher who was treated with great courtesy by Faithridge, and became his hanger-on. When threatened by the troops of Ch'in, Chao asked Faithridge for help. Hou, the one who had recommended Chu to Faithridge, suggested stealing the military tally, and Chu killed the commander with his gold hammer, so that Way's army was under Faithridge's command. In this way, Faithridge successfully saved Hantan, the capital of Chao.
* Pi Chin: Pi Chin (? - 257 B.C.), a commander of Way, killed by Chu.

* Ying Hou: Ying Hou (? -257 B.C.), a hermit who lived as a porter of Smooth Gate of the State of Way and became a hanger-on of Prince Faithridge.
* Prince of Way: referring to Prince Faithridge, one of the Four Childes in the Warring States period.
* like him in Ch'en: When Confucius travelled in the State of Ch'en, he had no supplies for several days.

## 鲁中送二从弟赴举之西京

鲁客向西笑，
君门若梦中。
霜凋逐臣发，
日忆明光宫。
复羡二龙去，
才华冠世雄。
平衢骋高足，
逸翰凌长风。
舞袖拂秋月，
歌筵闻早鸿。
送君日千里，
良会何由同。

## Seeing Off My Two Cousins to Capital to Take Grand Test

A guest like me does to west beam;
The court oft appears in my dream.
I grow gaunt and my hair grows gray
Because I miss it day after day.
How I admire your going west,
Your brilliance can outshine the best.
Like Pegasus across the plain,
Like Roc astride wind on the main!
Your sleeve stirs up an autumn breeze;
Your song attracts dawn-lit wild geese.

> I see you off to Grand Test there;
> When can we meet again and fare?

* Pegasus: a kind of horse from west of China, usually with wings in fairy tales, also known as sky-horse. In many cases it is used as a metaphor for a fine horse.
* Roc: a giant bird. According to *Sir Lush*, "There in North Sea is a fish called Minnow, whose body spans about a thousand miles. When transformed into a bird, it is called Roc, whose back spans about a thousand miles."
* wild goose: an undomesticated goose that is caring and responsible, taken as a symbol of benevolence, righteousness, good manner, wisdom and faith in Chinese culture.
* Grand Test: referring to imperial civil-service examinations for selecting talents to serve as meritocratic governmental officials, a system and practice initiated in the Han dynasty (202 B.C.- A.D. 220), formally begun in the Sui dynasty (A.D. 581 - A.D. 619), well-developed in the T'ang dynasty (A.D. 618 - A.D. 907) and abolished in the Late Ch'ing dynasty (A.D. 1636 - A.D. 1912). Those who passed the entree (chin shih) level were indeed given upper-echelon government appointments, and as a perk, they were generally allied by marriage to upper-crust families. In the eighteenth century, the Jesuits and their friend Voltaire recommended such a system for Europe as a safety valve for Europe's ossified social structure, which was soon overthrown by waves of aristocratic blood.

## 奉饯高尊师如贵道士传道箓毕归北海

道隐不可见，
灵书藏洞天。
吾师四万劫，
历世递相传。
别杖留青竹，
行歌蹑紫烟。
离心无远近，
长在玉京悬。

## Attending a Feast for Kao, a Wordist, to Return to North Sea After He Finishes Conducting a Wordist Conferment

The Wordist nobody can find;
And hidden is his *Book of Mind*.
My teacher's all pains undergone;
His wisdom's been to all passed on.
A bamboo stick helps him walk long;
In purple mist he sings a song.
Whether we're close or else apart,
On Mt. Fairy is hung my heart.

* the Wordist: a person believes in and practices Wordism, an important philosophical sect in China.
* *Book of Mind*: a spiritual book, written on purple jade in bronze characters.
* Mt. Fairy: used as a metaphor, any mountain for hermits or immortals.

## 金陵送张十一再游东吴

张翰黄花句，
风流五百年。
谁人今继作，
夫子世称贤。
再动游吴棹，
还浮入海船。
春光白门柳，
霞色赤城天。
去国难为别，
思归各未旋。
空馀贾生泪，
相顾共凄然。

## Seeing Off Chang Eleven to Tour East Wu Again

*The Day Lily Verse* by dear Han
Makes him five hundred years' first man.
Who will be the next first today?
You're praised as your talent does ray.
Now to tour Wu you'll row your boat;
Will you on the vast ocean float?
The White Gate willows don spring hue;
The red clouds have reddened the blue.
When leaving home I feel the pain;
When can I see my folks again?

Chia's tears have in vain dripped aground;
Now our sights are in sadness drowned.

* *The Day Lily Verse*: referring to Han Chang's verse *Miscellany*, which reads like this: "Good air corresponds with late spring; / The yard is in sunlight immersed. / The green twigs like emerald sway; / The day lilies are gold dispersed."
* great Han: referring to Han Chang, an official and a litterateur in the Western Chin dynasty. One late spring, the delicious perch in his hometown occurred to him, so he resigned and went back home, leaving behind his post in Loshine.

## 送纪秀才游越

海水不满眼，
观涛难称心。
即知蓬莱石，
却是巨鳌簪。
送尔游华顶，
令余发岛吟。
仙人居射的，
道士住山阴。
禹穴寻溪入，
云门隔岭深。
绿萝秋月夜，
相忆在鸣琴。

## Seeing Off Chi, a Showcharm, to Tour Yüeh

If one can't see all of the sea,
So satisfied he couldn't be.
Do you know the Fairy Isle stone
Was Giant Turtle's hairpin, as known?
To Floral Top I'll bring you soon;
A Yüeh ballad I'd like to croon.
The hermit does on top abide;
The Wordist lives on mountainside.
To find Worm's cave follow the creek;
Amid the hills Cloud Gate you seek.

The moonlit night chills the green vine;
If you miss me, play zither thine.

* showcharm: hsiuts'ai if transliterated, a talent recommended for official use through official examinations usually held every three years or a well-learned person in ancient China. A showcharm was well respected in the traditional Chinese society.
* Giant Turtle: referring to the turtle carrying Mt. Fairy. In Chinese mythology, there were fifteen giant turtles carrying five fairy mountains in turns in East Sea. But a giant man from the State of Giants on the sea caught six turtles and burnt them for divination. As a result, two mountains drifted to the extreme north and sank into the water, with only three fairy mountains left.
* Floral Top: the highest peak of Mt. Heaven, located in present-day Chechiang Province.
* Wordist: one who believes in or professes belief of Wordism, the doctrines declared by Laocius (571 B.C.- 471 B.C.).
* Worm's Cave: referring to where Worm, the founding lord of the Kingdom of Hsia, was buried.
* Cloud Gate: referring to a mountain in Chechiang.

# 送长沙陈太守二首

## Seeing Off Ch'en, Magistrate of Long Sand, Two Poems

### 其 一

长沙陈太守，
逸气凌青松。
英主赐五马，
本是天池龙。
湘水回九曲，
衡山望五峰。
荣君按节去，
不及远相从。

### No. 1

Ch'en, you are Long Sand's magistrate,
Straight like the pine tree and so great.
Five steeds His Majesty gave you,
As you're a dragon from the blue.
The Hsiang has nine bends, head to tail,
Viewing the five peaks of Mt. Scale.
You're going on your way, my friend,
I would escort you to the end!

* Long Sand: referring to Ch'angsha if transliterated, the capital city of present-day Hunan Province.
* dragon: a fabulous serpent-like giant winged animal that can change its girth and length, a totem of the Chinese nation, a symbol of benevolence and sovereignty in

Chinese culture.
* pine: a cone-bearing evergreen tree having needle-shaped leaves growing in clusters, a symbol of rectitude, fortitude and longevity in Chinese culture.
* the Hsiang: the most important river in today's Hunan Province.
* Mt. Scale: one of the Five Mountains in China, located in Hunan Province, along with Mt. Ever in Shanhsi, Mt. Arch in Shantung, Mt. Flora in Sha'anhsi, and Mt. Tower in Honan.

## 其 二

七郡长沙国，
南连湘水滨。
定王垂舞袖，
地窄不回身。
莫小二千石，
当安远俗人。
洞庭乡路远，
遥羡锦衣春。

## No. 2

Seven counties of Long Sand, lo,
Are linked in south to the Hsiang's blue.
King Peace, who liked Sleeve Waving dance,
Said this place was too small to prance.
A small pay don't you look down on;
This lord can settle everyone.
Though Cavehall's your home far away,
I do admire your bright array!

* Long Sand: referring to Ch'angsha if transliterated, a vassal state in the Han dynasty and now the capital city of present-day Hunan Province.
* King Peace: King Peace of Long Sand (202 B.C.- A.D. 7), the first vassal state in Han, specifics unknown.
* Cavehall: a lake in present-day Hunan Province.

## 送杨燕之东鲁

关西杨伯起,
汉日旧称贤。
四代三公族,
清风播人天。
夫子华阴居,
开门对玉莲。
何事历衡霍,
云帆今始还。
君坐稍解颜,
为君歌此篇。
我固侯门士,
谬登圣主筵。
一辞金华殿,
蹭蹬长江边。
二子鲁门东,
别来已经年。
因君此中去,
不觉泪如泉。

## Seeing Off Yan Yang to East Lu

Poch'i Yang in West during Han
Was regarded as a sage man.
In four generations, three wise
Premiers from the Yang's did rise.
You are from the town Floral Shade,

Your door facing Lotus of Jade.
For what to the hills did you go
And came back but today like so?
Sit down, do have a rest a while;
I'll sing a song to you beguile.
From a peer's household I descend;
The Lord's feast I did fain attend.
Once I did leave the Golden Court,
And to the Yangtze there resort.
East of Lu Gate I have two sons;
It's years since I saw my dear ones.
I miss them as you're going there;
In tears the distance I can't bear.

* Poch'i Yang: a righteous and upright official scholar in the Han dynasty.
* Floral Shade: a town 120 kilometers from Long Peace, an important passage in T'ang, situated in the northside of Mt. Flora, hence its name.
* Lotus of Jade: a peak of Mt. Flora.
* the Golden Court: a palace in Non-end Palace in the Han dynasty; a metaphor for any court in later dynasties.
* the Yangtze: the lower reaches of the Long River, from Nanking to the estuary in Shanghai.
* Lu Gate: the gateway to Lu.

# 送 蔡 山 人

我本不弃世，
世人自弃我。
一乘无倪舟，
八极纵远舵。
燕客期跃马，
唐生安敢讥。
采珠勿惊龙，
大道可暗归。
故山有松月，
迟尔玩清晖。

# Seeing Off Ts'ai, the Hermit

It's not I that from the world flee;
It's the world that does reject me.
I am now in an aimless boat,
Unto Eight Bounds afloat, afloat.
You jump on your horse, there astride;
Dare Chü T'ang still your life deride?
Don't stir the blue when seeking pearls;
The Great Word on its own unfurls.
Atop the hills stand moonlit pines;
You can play there while the moon shines.

\* Eight Bounds: eight directions or farmost places.
\* Chü T'ang: the one who derided Tse Ts'ai and predicted the latter had forty three

years more to live.
* pearl: a smooth, lustrous, usually white and bluish-gray, calcareous concretion deposited in layers around a central nucleus in the shells of various mollusks or oysters, and largely used as a gem, medicine or given as a gift, a metaphor for the dearest one, a representation of nobility, purity and dignity in Chinese culture.
* the Great Word: the Word, the Creator, the beginning of everything.

## 送萧三十一之鲁中兼问稚子伯禽

六月南风吹白沙，  
吴牛喘月气成霞。  
水国郁蒸不可处，  
时炎道远无行车。  
夫子如何涉江路？  
云帆袅袅金陵去。  
高堂倚门望伯鱼，  
鲁中正是趋庭处。  
我家寄在沙丘傍，  
三年不归空断肠。  
君行既识伯禽子，  
应驾小车骑白羊。

## Seeing Off Hsiao Thirteen to Mid-Lu, Who May Go See My Son There

Sixth moon, a southern wind blows up white sand;  
A cow in Wu breathes air into clouds grand.  
The water realm damp, one can't there abide;  
It's hot! It's far! There's no cart for a ride.  
How will you go back? Go downstream you will!  
The sails in white clouds leave the Golden Hill.  
Your parents gaze at the door for their son;  
Mid-Lu's where Confucius taught his dear one.  
My home is far there, beside the sand knoll;  
I've been out for three years, so sad my soul.

> You may go see my son now you depart;
> He'd be playing, riding a goat or cart.

* Wu: a southern vassal state of Chough.
* Confucius: Confucius (551 B.C. - 479 B.C.), a renowned thinker, educator and statesman in the Spring and Autumn period, born in the State of Lu, who was the founder of Confucianism and who has exerted profound influence on Chinese culture for more than two thousand years. He is one of the few leaders who based their philosophy on the virtues that are required for the day-to-day living. His philosophy centered on personal and governmental morality, correctness of social relationships, justice and sincerity.
* Confucius taught his dear one: dear one referring to Confucius' son, Conglee, styled First Carp. This is an allusion to Confoucious' teaching of his son, a dialogue between Ch'enk'ang, Confucius' disciple and Conglee. As a chapter of the *Analect* recounts, Ch'enk'ang asked Conlee: "Are you given special teaching?" Conlee replied: "No. One day he stood in the classroom, and when I passed, he asked me: 'Are you learning *Poems*?' I answered: 'No.' 'Without learning *Poems*, you've nothing to say.' So, I retired to read *Poems*. Another day, he stood in the classroom, and when I passed, he asked: 'Are you learning rites?' I answered: 'No.' 'Without learning rites, you have nowhere to stand.' So, I retired to learn rites. I've had just these two teachings." Ch'enkang retired while remarking with glee: "Asking one question, I got three answers. *Poems*, rites, and the teacher impartial to his son."
* goat: a hollow-horned ruminant (genus *Capra*) of rocky and mountainous regions, related to the sheep and including wild and domesticated forms.

# 送杨山人归嵩山

我有万古宅，
嵩阳玉女峰。
长留一片月，
挂在东溪松。
尔去掇仙草，
菖蒲花紫茸。
岁晚或相访，
青天骑白龙。

## Sending Off Yang, a Hermit, to Mt. Tower

I have an estate that's age-old,
Where Mt. Tower does Jade Maid uphold.
For e'er the disc of moon would beam
O'er the green pines by the east stream.
Now to cull magic herbs you'll go;
The sedge blossoms in purple hue.
Someday, we may into godhood pry
And ride a white dragon sky-high.

* Mt. Tower: one of the five most famous mountains in China. It is in today's Honan Province, the center of China. It is one of the five sanctuaries of Wordism, and the abode of God of Mt. Tower worshipped by Han Chinese, with an area of 450 square kilometers, consisting of Mt. Greatroom and Mt. Smallroom, having 72 peaks, 350 meters above sea level at the lowest and 1,512 meters at the highest.
* Jade Maid: a peak on Mt. Tower.

* the moon: the planet of the earth, which appears at night and gives off shining silvery light, an image of purity and solitude in Chinese culture.
* sedge: a grasslike cyperaceous herb with flowers densely clustered in spikes; widely distributed in marshy places.
* white dragon: a dragon in white in Chinese mythology, often regarded as River God.

# 送殷淑三首
## Seeing Off Shu Yin, Three Poems

### 其 一

海水不可解，
连江夜为潮。
俄然浦屿阔，
岸去酒船遥。
惜别耐取醉，
鸣榔且长谣。
天明尔当去，
应便有风飘。

### No.1

Sea water you cannot divide;
At night upstream it throws a tide.
Suddenly wide get sea and shore;
The wine boat off is seen no more.
It's good to get drunk at good-bye;
Just sing a song and the oar ply.
At daybreak you will rise to go;
An easy wind to you will blow.

## 其 二

白鹭洲前月，
天明送客回。
青龙山后日，
早出海云来。
流水无情去，
征帆逐吹开。
相看不忍别，
更进手中杯。

## No. 2

O'er Egret Shoal the moon is bright;
It'll see you off when dawn sheds light.
The sun behind Blue Dragon hides
And rises early from sea tides.
The flowing water will be gone,
While to your sail a wind blows on.
I hate to see you go, friend mine;
Do drink your cup, do drink your wine.

* Egret Shoal: 4 kilometers from Gold Hill, now the biggest park in the southern area of today's Nanking.
* Blue Dragon: Mt. Blue Dragon, a mountain 15.25 kilometers from Gold Hill, i.e. today's Nanking.

## 其　三

痛饮龙邻下，
灯青月复寒。
醉歌惊白鹭，
半夜起沙滩。

## No. 3

We drink like mad in the bamboo;
The lantern grows cold and looks blue.
Our song does egrets there surprise
At night, up from Sand Shoal they rise.

* egret: a heron characterized, in the breeding season, by long and loose plumes drooping over the tail, usually white plumage.
* Sand Shoal: unidentified, probably a shoal in the Yangtze River.

## 送岑征君归鸣皋山

岑公相门子,
雅望归安石。
奕世皆夔龙,
中台竟三拆。
至人达机兆,
高揖九州伯。
奈何天地间,
而作隐沦客。
贵道能全真,
潜辉卧幽邻。
探元入窅默,
观化游无垠。
光武有天下,
严陵为故人。
虽登洛阳殿,
不屈巢由身。
余亦谢明主,
今称偃蹇臣。
登高览万古,
思与广成邻。
蹈海宁受赏,
还山非问津。
西来一摇扇,
共拂元规尘。

# Seeing Off Ts'en, a Recruit, to Mt. Chirping Bog

A premier's son, enjoying fame,
In grace, with Anshi you're the same.
Each generation sees the best;
Three of you belong to the crest.
A sign shows when a saint comes down;
You aim high and bow to the crown.
Lo, sky and earth, the world entire,
See you as a recluse retire.
The Word is whole as it is true;
A dragon hides deep in the blue.
We'd better seek what is profound
Across the cosmos without bound.
When Lightmight ascended the throne,
Your friend, Yan, would be left alone.
When you rose high in Loshine Hall,
Retired, you would not bow at all.
His Majesty I thanked and left;
Now I'm a proud man though bereft.
I think of the past now climbing high,
I'd live with Goodharvest nearby.
Rather than be favored you'd die
To serve the court you would not try.
When west wind comes I'll myself fan,
Clean of vain dust, I'm a pure man.

---

\* Mt. Chirping Bog: a mountain in Luhun County, i.e. today's Mt. Tower County (Sung

County), Honan Province.
* the Word: referring to Tao if transliterated, the most significant and profoundest concept in Chinese philosophy. The Word is fully elucidated in *The Word and the World*, the single book that Laocius wrote all his wisdom into. Its importance can be seen in this verse: "The Word is void, but its use is infinite. O deep! It seems to be the root of all things."
* cosmos: the world or universe considered as a system, perfect in order and arrangement, opposed to chaos.
* dragon: a fabulous serpent-like giant winged animal that can change its girth and length, a symbol of benevolence and sovereignty in Chinese culture.
* Lightmight: the posthumous title of Hsiu Liu (6 B.C.- A.D. 57), who re-established the governance of Han and started the reign of the Eastern Han.
* Yan: referring to Tsuling Yan (39 B.C.- A.D. 41), a renowned hermit in the Han dynasty, who declined Lightmight's offer of a post in the government and chose to live in seclusion in the Richspring Hills.
* Goodharvest: Sir Goodharvest, a Wordist in Lord Yellow's age. Lord Yellow visited him for ideas of governance when the latter was practicing the Word at Mt. Hollow.

## 送范山人归泰山

鲁客抱白鹤，
别余往泰山。
初行若片云，
杳在青崖间。
高高至天门，
日观近可攀。
云山望不及，
此去何时还。

## Seeing Off Fan, the Hermit, Back to Mt. Arch

From Lu, a white crane in arms, you
Will climb Arch, having said adieu.
The crags fly clear like flakes of snow;
The path's lost while ahead you go.
High above, Heaven's Gate is there;
Climb the Sunview Peak if you dare.
Some mist-peaks are too steep to climb,
When can you come back then, what time?

* Mt. Arch: one of the Five Mountains in China. There are five especially sacred mountains in China, one for each of the four directions and one at the center. Mt. Arch, in the east, is the most revered of these mountains, as its name may suggest, and its summit is the destination of many pilgrims. Mt. Arch complex includes many lower ridges and summits.
* crane: one of a family of large, long-necked, long-legged, heronlike birds allied to the

rails, a symbol of integrity and longevity in Chinese culture, only second to the phoenix in cultural importance.

* Arch: Mt. Arch, the most sacred of the Five Mountains in China. As legend goes, 72 sovereigns in prehistoric China made sacrifices to the god of the mountain and according to historical records, 12 emperors made their sacrifices from Emperor First of the Ch'in dynasty to Highfather (Chienlung) of the Ch'ing dynasty.
* Heaven's Gate: South Heaven's Gate, one of the three gates bearing the name Heaven's Gate in Mt. Arch.
* the Sunview Peak: the highest peak of Mt. Arch.